JURASSIC CARNAGE

THREE TALES OF CREATURE-FEATURE HORROR

JULIAN MICHAEL CARVER

SEVEREDPRESS

JURASSIC CARNAGE

JURASSIC CARNAGE

In the expanse of the ocean, a drug cartel faces off against the Coast Guard—and a hungry megalodon lurking beneath the waves. Then, at a truck-stop diner, tensions run high as a swarm of angry murder hornets attack, trapping the customers inside! Finally, deep in the forest, a group of hikers are fighting for their lives—pursued by a bloodthirsty theropod long thought to be extinct.

Jurassic Carnage and Other Monster Tales is the debut collection by American science-fiction writer Julian Michael Carver. The stories contained in this collection were previously published as individual releases called *Creature Features*. This collection also features an unreleased tale—*Jurassic Carnage*.

Julian Michael Carver is a Scribe Award nominated author and a proud member of the International Association of Media Tie-In Writers. He is known for his tales regarding dinosaurs and prehistoric monsters.

MEGALODON RIPTIDE

1

"Are you blind, Davis? Hit those assholes!"

Cassidy Davis ignored her employer's brusque demeanor, emptying the magazine of her Beretta Px4 Storm at the oncoming U.S. Coast Guard Interceptor, wincing as muzzle flashes burst in front of her like a fireworks finale. The speedboat she was on lurched unexpectedly, sending all of her poorly aimed shots into the roiling waves of the Pacific.

Fetid ocean water nipped at her face, forcing her to brush her soaked brown hair away from her eyes. She spat out the saltwater as she looked up, just in time to see the stern look of her shadowy employer.

"Where the hell did you learn to shoot, Davis?" asked Nikki Salerno, the boss of the Salerno Cartel.

"Well tell Xavier to take it easy on those waves!" Cassidy yelled over the boat's blaring engines, undeterred by her superior's chastising outburst. "There's no use going so fast if he just wrecks into one of the burning boats!"

"I hired you because I thought you'd come in handy," Nikki grumbled, jamming another magazine into her Heckler and Koch MP7 submachine gun. "All you've done so far is piss me off! And now everything's gone to hell! The whole crime syndicate's fallen apart! You *at least* remembered the money, didn't you?"

"The briefcase is up with Xavier," Cassidy grumbled impatiently.

She'll try to do me in the first chance she gets, Cassidy thought, anticipating a lethal showdown as soon as they cleared the smoking field of floating debris. *I'll have to make my move before then...*

"Well at least you did one thing right," came the loathsome reply.

Cassidy watched as the crime lord successfully readied her weapon, whirling around in her black leather jacket over the edge of their fleeing speedboat and presumed to rattle off more rounds at the oncoming cutter. In the distance, their former drug headquarters – an abandoned oil rig – burned like a funeral pyre from Coast Guard helicopter air missile attacks. Rusted ladders and support structures rained down in a fiery shower to the ocean below. Additional henchmen descended to the tethered docks to escape, only to discover all the evacuation boats had already been deployed or set ablaze in the maelstrom of gunfire.

In the ocean surrounding the burning structure, dozens of additional boats sat ablaze from the hour long shootout. Coast Guard cutters and drug vessels alike were destroyed in the conflict. Bodies of seamen and rogue gunmen drifted in the current among the flaming ships, bullet riddled but kept afloat by life vests. By the time Nikki and Cassidy boarded one of the final boats, there were no attack helicopters left in the sky, and only a few Interceptors deployed by the U.S. Coast Guard remained. Both sides had been depleted to only a few combatants. The window of escape would be thin, Cassidy realized. Coast Guard reinforcements were bound to arrive soon, turning the tide in favor of the United States military.

"*Incoming!*" Nikki yelled, firing away with her MP7.

Two Interceptors took chase to the Cartel craft. Nikki's second-in-command, a rather unpleasant enforcer named Xavier, drove the speedboat swiftly through the flaming obstacles, occasionally yelling obscenities at the precarious situation. One other gunman, a disgruntled old-timer named Leon sat in the back of the boat with them, removing a GM-94 grenade launcher out from its black Pelican case.

We may be the only survivors, Cassidy thought, quickly loading another clip into her Beretta. *Most of the others probably died on the rig!*

Leon popped up for a moment from cover, carrying with him the grenade launcher. Pressing down on the trigger, the weapon launched an impressive shot at the closest Interceptor. The blast caught the cutter in the bow, crippling the craft's ability to give further pursuit. The explosion burst the cutter into flame, sending hot shrapnel flying like an active volcano all over the scorched deck. Screams from burning seamen yelped from the ship as they leaped from the stern, perishing beneath the green waves, their fates ambiguous.

"One down, boss!" Leon cackled behind his white unkempt beard, blowing on the barrel of the grenade launcher.

"Don't get cocky, Leon," Nikki muttered, fidgeting with another magazine from her utility belt. "There's still one left! Xavier, there's another one of our boats. Link up with them and we'll double our odds of getting out of here!"

"Right, boss!" came the gruff reply from the cabin.

Xavier pulled their craft next to the other cartel speedboat that was escaping the burning graveyard of ships. Cassidy glanced over the railing, unable to discern any of the henchmen due to their ski-masks and thick trench coats. She decided most of them had to be low-level thugs who were lucky enough to escape the docks, and were concurrently making the same play at escape. One of the masked gunmen turned and shouted in their direction from the speedboat's bow, pointing toward the oncoming cutter.

"The last one's not gonna give up chase!" bellowed a large muscular man carrying an AK-47 assault rifle. "Let's unload on his ass or we're fish bait!"

"I thought you'd never ask!" Nikki laughed maniacally.

Both cartel boats began to fire at the oncoming cutter, sending bullets whizzing over the turbulent waves. Blinded by the afternoon sun, Cassidy winced as most of her rounds struck the waves surrounding the Interceptor, even as it closed the gap to barely forty yards. Her poor aim went unnoticed; Nikki Salerno was too preoccupied spraying and praying to notice her subordinate's lack of accuracy.

"*Look out!*" one of the henchmen from the adjacent boat bellowed, frantically trying to correct his jammed firearm. Several other goons in the back pointed and shrieked. Cassidy followed their gaze, realizing what troubled them.

Oh shit!

In an instant, a coast guard seaman arrived at the Interceptor's front machine gun, sending a wave of gunfire raining down on the secondary cartel boat. Bullets cut through the air, tearing through all of the henchmen on the deck, killing them instantly. Several rounds penetrated the cabin, striking the driver and forcing the boat to veer left, away from its present trajectory. Seconds later, the cartel boat crashed into a downed Coast Guard helicopter. An explosion followed, engulfing the cartel boat and chopper wreckage in a goblet of flame. The blast was so volatile, Cassidy could feel the tingle of warmth teasing her soaked cheek as her boat streaked past the wreckage.

"*Shit!*" Nikki cried, slamming a balled fist down on the railing. "There goes our last lifeline. We're next if we don't do something. Leon, can you range him from here with that grenade launcher?"

"I'll try," Leon replied, rising from the deck – only to be greeted by an incoming storm of .50 caliber machine gun fire.

"Get *dow* –" Nikki's cry went interrupted.

The burst of concentrated machine gun fire crashed into their speedboat. Cassidy covered her ears as the *ting-tang-tick* cacophony of bullets pounded the rusted metal siding. In the cabin ahead, she could see Xavier ducking down as the windshield burst into shards as the boat cleared the debris field and entered a stretch of open ocean. Several crude drug cartel emblems and posters on the wall were eviscerated by the bullets, and a few of the hanging life vests were punctured and left in disarray.

Through the unfolding chaos being unleashed to her speedboat, Cassidy turned to her left, seeing that Nikki had inserted another magazine into her machine gun. To her right, Leon was still hunkered down, expecting decapitation if he popped up too soon from cover. The four of them were hardly a match against an operational .50 caliber machine gun.

Suddenly the gunfire ceased, leaving only the sounds of their propeller behind as it chopped through ocean water. In the cabin, Xavier hesitantly reached for the wheel, staring out through the shattered glass at the ocean ahead, before casting a hesitant glance back at their pursuers.

"He must be reloading!" Xavier called, quickly searching for a weapon. "Their boat's getting closer! He'll wipe us out with the next blast!"

"Leon, grenade his seaworthy ass so we can dip out!" Nikki commanded.

"How do we know he's just not waiting until I pop back up?" came the greasy old man's stern reply.

"How about do it or I'm putting one in your old skull, you old buffoon!" Nikki shot back, gesturing to her weapon. "We don't have time for what-ifs, asshole."

"Wait, Leon," Cassidy pleaded, "Maybe we can just *outrun –*"

"Shut up, *bitch!*" Nikki cut her off, waving her leather gloved fist in Cassidy's face. "Leon, do it! Do it *now!*"

Whispering a prolific array of colorful swear words, Leon checked his weapon and quickly arose from cover. Cassidy peered over the edge, watching as her partner fired off another grenade round – with equally lethal precision as his first attempt. The round exploded on the gunner at the machine gun port, killing the soldier and disabling the Interceptor's bow. Water rushed through the fractured opening as a few fortunate soldiers jumped off the Interceptor's stern. Soon the boat was a sinking speck in the distance, as was the burning oil rig and the fiery graveyard of ships.

"We made it!" Nikki smiled, looking out over the stretches of waves at the remnants of her crumbling drug manufacturing plant. "Looks like we're the only ones that got away. Surprised we managed to take on an entire Coast Guard flotilla with just the weapons we had at the rig! I always said we needed more guns! I'm gonna miss that place. It was the perfect spot to run the operation until the coasties caught wind of us. Nice shootin', Leon."

Leon offered a friendly nod, wiping off his greasy brow. Cassidy sensed palpable tension between her employer and the older man. She had worked under Nikki Salerno for several months, and had known her to be a stern leader. She had also known her to occasionally threaten the lives of her own cartel subordinates – a trait that made her both respected and feared.

"Xavier, do you have the case?" Nikki asked.

"Yeah, boss. A little dinged up, but still in good shape."

The large muscular tattooed thug lumbered out from the cabin, walking with an odd gait that Cassidy sensed caused him great agony. In his right hand, he gripped a silver briefcase that looked to Cassidy like it belonged in an old James Bond film. Nikki took the case, gasping at Xavier's hand.

"Shit, you've been shot!"

"Not that bad," Xavier replied, gently padding his wounds with a filthy rag. "One just grazed my arm. The two that hit my leg are worse, but I can manage. I don't think they hit any arteries, but I'm sure as shit no doctor."

"You should hope not," Nikki frowned, gesturing at the deck floor. "You're bleeding all over the deck! You better not attract any sharks. You know how I hate those. Okay, time to make sure it's all accounted for."

Nikki plopped the large briefcase on an old wooden table, used her combination to unlock it and clicked the latches up one after the other before opening the top. The drug lord smiled down at the result; a compartment full of neatly accounted stacks of hundred dollar bills. Judging by the numeric value imprinted on the money straps, Cassidy assumed there was at least ten million dollars stashed in the case.

"It's not as much as I could've had if the coasties hadn't arrived when they did," Nikki cursed, "but coupled with what I have stashed back in Sacramento, it'll be enough to get another division up and running again."

"How much is there, boss?" Leon asked, leaning in with a toothy grin.

"Enough," Nikki said coldly, slamming the briefcase shut and locking it with her secret combination. "Xavier, get us out of here! I want to be in Californian waters by nightfall. It was a miracle none of the blasts hit our fuel tank. Do you think we have enough gas to get to the mainland?"

"Pretty damn close," Xavier said. "I reckon we'll make it."

"If not, we'll just hijack some do-gooder's boat," Nikki chuckled, handing the briefcase back to Xavier. "I don't think they'll miss it too much where they'll be going."

Cassidy bit her tongue, wanting to offer rebuttal. Nikki's regard for human life was virtually nonexistent.

"Something to say, Davis?" Nikki shot her a glare, sensing her employee's discontent.

"Nothing," Cassidy replied, forcing a phony smile of compliance.

Xavier cast aside the rickety bullet riddled cabin door and arrived at the wheel, throwing the briefcase carelessly on a table. Quickly surveying the dashboard console for signs of damage, he gave Nikki a thumbs up and pressed down on the throttle, sending them ahead in the direction of the California shoreline.

Cassidy holstered her sidearm, grateful to be alive as they blazed away from the war zone.

As she turned toward the bow and checked herself over for injuries, a giant dorsal fin arose from the ocean, following the cartel boat before diving back below.

Unbeknownst to the four cartel members, they were being followed.

2

Cassidy looked over the stretches of ocean as the cartel boat tore through the waves at breakneck speed. In the cabin, she could hear Nikki cursing as she counted her money, angered that there was still room for more bills before the briefcase was packed. Xavier remained at the wheel, trying to put them at a California beach before nightfall. By now the sun was sinking near the horizon. Cassidy assumed they had two hours at the most of daylight.

As Leon's second hand cigarette smoke wafted into her nostrils, she gagged, turning away from the unsavory scent.

"Oops, sorry about that, Davis," Leon muttered, quickly adjusting his smoking position to save his friend from the fumes. "Didn't realize the wind was blowing that way."

"Don't worry about it," Cassidy replied, casting a cautious look back at the cabin before she continued. "So, you thinkin' what I'm thinkin'?"

"What?" Leon asked, flicking the small cigarette into the churning waves.

"That Nikki will kill us before we ever make it to shore?"

Leon shot a subtle look at the cabin before answering.

"I would say it's a high probability," Leon said calmly. "I'm sure by now the Coast Guard or some three lettered agency has all of our pictures from those helicopters or satellite feeds. Somehow a mole must've infiltrated the rig, and probably gave the authorities all of our information. Technically speaking, if we're discovered on the mainland, we could be loose ends. No honor among thieves, after all. Obviously, Xavier's safe. She idolizes him. There were rumors they were even sleeping together."

"So what's our play here?" Cassidy asked. "Wait for them to cap us or do something about it?"

"I'm still weighing the options," Leon admitted. "With Xavier wounded, he might not be hard. But ever since Nikki went into the cabin, have you noticed they've been speaking in hushed tones? Nikki hasn't turned her back to us since we left the rig. I'd say we probably don't have long until they make their power play."

That sent a chill up Cassidy's spine.

"Okay, when do you want to make our move?"

"I'd say about now would be great," Leon said. "But all I have is a grenade launcher. That won't do us very good seeing as how we still want the boat to work. You'll have to do it. How many bullets do you have left?"

"Barely a clip."

"That'll do. Pop Nikki first and then do Xavier, since he's facing away anyway. I can figure out how to drive the boat. Then we'll be home free."

Cassidy shuddered, but returned his serious gaze with a firm nod.

"Here goes nothing."

Leon gave her a discreet wink as Cassidy turned toward the boat's cabin. Through the shattered windows, she could see Nikki still thumbing through the wads of cash. Xavier remained rooted at the driver position, guiding the cartel boat slowly toward the East where California remained somewhere over the horizon.

She felt the pattern of the pistol grip digging into her hand as she neared the doorway to the cabin. A bead of sweat slipped over her hand. In all her time in Nikki's servitude, she had never grown the courage to confront her on any issue, due to her employer's deadly temper. Failure to secure the boat now would meet with deadly consequences.

"Those greedy bastards," Nikki muttered to Xavier, thumbing through a wad of c-notes. "Xavier, I'm tellin' you some of those new recruits you found from LA shorted us. Those cadavers are probably up in smoke by now on the rig. Good riddance, filthy robbers."

"You were right, boss," Xavier replied, eyes locked on the oncoming ocean as his hands gripped the wheel. "I should just learn to trust your killer instincts. Then maybe we'd be making off with more stacks right now. When we assemble a new crew together, I'll be more cautious during the hiring process."

"No need for that," Nikki smiled, placing a rubber band around a stack. "We'll just be more diligent about doing away with the trouble makers."

Cassidy turned, shooting a look at Leon. The old-timer had already lit up another cigarette, puffing as he looked out the rear of the boat. Shooting her a discreet nod, she saw him ruffle his eyebrow, signifying that he was also listening in on their murderous conversation.

Taking a deep breath, she turned into the cabin, keeping her grip on the pistol behind her back.

"Excuse me, *Nikk –*"

Cassidy's words were cut off as the world around her shook with sudden volatility. Her forehead struck the door frame of the cabin as her body crumpled to the deck. Inside the cabin, she could see Nikki tumble to the floor as well, knocking over her briefcase full of money and sending the wads of cash to the floor. Xavier caught himself by grabbing the wheel of the boat, forcing the craft to veer left.

"*Augh!*" Cassidy cried, turning around, rubbing her forehead.

She caught sight of the rear of the boat, where Leon had also been knocked to the floor. Still puffing away angrily at a cigarette, Leon staggered clumsily to his feet, quickly pointing at Cassidy's hand. Cassidy understood, quickly sheathing her pistol to avoid suspicion. Right now, there was an even bigger problem than the cutthroat drug lord.

Something had rocked the boat.

"What the shit was that?" Nikki spat, using the ledge of the table in the cabin to pull herself back to her feet.

Beside her, Xavier resumed command at the wheel, setting the craft on an adjusted route to the mainland before turning back to his employer.

"How the hell should I know?" Xavier grumbled. "Davis, you got any ideas?"

"No," Cassidy said as she finished discreetly securing the pistol in its holster. "For a second, I thought the Coast Guard was using torpedoes on us."

"*Torpedoes?*" Nikki spat, arching her brows. "Get real, Davis. It's the Coast Guard, not a naval submarine. Even if they did have torpedoes, they wouldn't waste one on our pissant little speedboat. It might've been a walrus."

"That was one hell of a walrus," Xavier added. "If that's what it was. *Ah,* shit! Uh, boss, we got a problem here!"

"What?" Nikki asked, a hint of impatience in her tone.

"Whatever that thing was," Xavier began, "it did something to our propeller. We're slowing down. Pretty soon we'll just be floating here. We'll be sitting ducks for the Coast Guard reinforcements..."

Nikki ran up to the control console as Cassidy walked into the cabin. The damage lights and warning indicators had the front console lit up like a Christmas tree. Nikki slammed her fist down next to the steering wheel, before racing to pick up all the spilled money.

"We have to do something, Xavier!" she grumbled, collecting the funds on the table. "We can't just wait here for the damn choppers to pick us up! Can't you do something?"

"What do you want me to do?" Xavier spouted angrily. "I can operate a basic speedboat! I can't repair our propulsion problems in open water!"

"Well someone think of something, dammit!" Nikki roared as she slammed the briefcase shut. "Davis, take this and double check my math. We should have close to nine million there. Make sure there is at least that."

"Okay but what about *th* –"

Cassidy's question was silenced by the slam of the cabin door. She turned back to the stern of the boat as Nikki and Xavier began arguing in the cabin about how to amend their dire situation. Leon was halfway through his next cigarette butt.

"The hell was that, Davis?" he said as she arrived next to him.

"I'm sorry," Cassidy replied, cracking open the briefcase as she began to count the bills. "I couldn't do it. By the time I got back up they were already looking at me."

"I'm not talking about that," Leon winced, blowing smoke. "I mean what the hell hit our boat. And I heard that dialogue in there. I'm tellin' you, Davis – it ain't no walrus."

"You sure?" Cassidy laughed, removing a rubber band. "Actually, I was thinking we just hit a sandbar. I used to surf in my early twenties. There's actually quite a few hidden sandbars out this way."

"But this far out?" Leon smirked. "I doubt it. No, Davis. Something big hit us. I'm talking whale big, if not bigger."

"Now you're just trying to freak me out, you old bastard," Cassidy chuckled.

"Well it's big enough to screw up the propeller," Leon said, looking over the edge.

"You honestly think a whale knocked into our boat?" Cassidy asked, flipping through another stack. "I'd be more likely to believe a great white shark."

"Could be," Leon muttered ominously. "Could be."

Great white shark attacks had been occurring more frequently in the Pacific Ocean in recent years. A year earlier, a surfer, Terry Wolf, was attacked and killed by a twenty-foot-long great white. Having been missing for weeks, his death was finally confirmed when his head washed up in California. Detectives were able to confirm the identity through dental records. The idea of a great white shark big enough to rock their boat sent a chill up her spine.

"So, what are we gonna do about the gruesome twosome?" Leon asked, breaking through her thoughts. "They're probably thinking of knifing us as we speak."

"I think with the propeller acting up," Cassidy replied, "the two of them have more on their minds."

She cast a look back to the cabin. Through the windows, she could see Nikki berating her subordinate as Xavier tried to troubleshoot the control console. Some of the words bled through the open window, allowing Cassidy to hear a small segment of the conversation.

"Large enough to..." Xavier's voice began intermediately as he pointed to a sonar system. "Comin' back around... right for us!"

Something about the scene alarmed Cassidy. For one, as large and muscular of a man as Xavier was, she had never seen him this frightened by something before. Through the glass, she watched as he frantically worked through the boat controls and settings, trying to get their craft to move. By now, the boat had come to a complete stop, drifting hopelessly on the surface of the Pacific.

"Leon, something's not right," Cassidy said, facing the cabin. "I've never seen Xavier this worked up before. Nikki's really goin' nuts too. I think we may be in for –"

"Davis, shut the hell up," Leon said abruptly.

"*What?*"

"Look!"

Cassidy turned to her friend, watching as Leon's skin turned pale. His hand trembled as it gripped the deck rail. His jaw dangled open, letting his cigarette fall to the waves below.

"Leon, what the *fu* –"

Cassidy gritted her teeth as she pinpointed the oncoming disastrous visual, biting her tongue. Ignoring the pain, she stood up over the deck next to Leon. Fear kept her rooted in her position, and she found herself unable to look away from the deep terror that approached.

A hundred yards away in the waves of the Pacific, a massive blue dorsal fin cut through the surface of the ocean. Parting water like the front of an icebreaker, the dorsal fin swerved about in an arc motion as the fish adjusted its trajectory to head toward the neutralized craft.

Cassidy felt her one hand gripping the rail tightly, while the other clenched the closed briefcase handle.

"It's a... great white," she muttered, as she heard Nikki and Xavier walking up behind them.

"It's too big to be a great white," Xavier added, standing on the other side of Cassidy. "It's a... a..."

"It's a megalodon!" Leon cried, stumbling backward in fright.

"It's gonna ram us!" Nikki shrieked as the large shadow engulfed the boat.

The megalodon had quickly closed the gap from a hundred yards to fifty, parting the waves with its imminent and disastrous approach. The height of the waves wrought by the creature's massive fin created a rift in the ocean, lifting the speedboat at an odd angle as the meg cut the distance to only twenty yards in a matter of seconds.

The dorsal fin grew large – so large it blocked out the sun. Cassidy's heart raced as the boat was lifted up onto the first wave. In an instant, the dorsal fin struck the edge of the boat, while simultaneously the megalodon's upper body rocked the bottom of the craft.

"*Ugh!*"

Cassidy felt Xavier land on his ass beside her, as Nikki's cries of terror masked the swelling churn of the wave. As she lost control of her balance, she felt her feet leave the boat as she went airborne. Hauling the briefcase full of drug money with her, Cassidy closed her eyes as the cold water enveloped her, and suddenly she could not escape one crippling thought.

She was in open water with the largest predator she had ever seen.

3

As the cold water of the Pacific rolled around her in an aquatic frenzy, Cassidy felt herself being pulled down by the meg's dominant riptide. Bubbles shot toward her from all directions, adding to her disorientation as she spiraled farther down into the gloom.

Oh shit! Oh shit!

Recycling profanities on a loop through her mind was the only way she found herself able to self-sooth. She had been in open water before, and even had a brush with a tiger-shark once in her youth. But this situation was something else entirely – something, she decided, was straight out of her darkest nightmares.

Holding onto the silvery briefcase wasn't helping matters either. The weight of the heavy luggage helped the relentless ocean to haul her farther down. Above, through the swarm of bubbles brought forth by the meg's colossal tail, Cassidy saw the speedboat getting farther away as the ocean sucked her down.

They would've left my ass if I didn't have the cash in hand, Cassidy mused, her long hair floating in front of her, blocking her view of the watercraft. *Hell, the shark screwed up the propeller. They couldn't leave if they wanted to...*

Through her blurry vision, she turned to her right – the last known direction of the megalodon. The massive creature had vanished, leaving only contrails of bubbles fizzling to the surface as evidence of its arrival. Cassidy struggled to kick her way back up to the surface, but the briefcase weighed her down, despite her strongest kicks.

Come on, dammit! That thing will be comin' back!

Through the distorted wave refraction above, she could see Leon and Xavier's faces looking down, trying to find her. Even over the churning ebb and flow of the current, Cassidy could hear Nikki's angry tirade. It was no surprise that the drug lord was more concerned about her sunken treasure than her expendable shipmate.

That greedy bitch!

The arguing continued above. Leon made an attempt to assuage Nikki's anger, only to receive what looked like an angry slap across the face, knocking him out of view. Cassidy looked down at the briefcase as she felt the crunch of her lungs.

Screw this! I'd rather deal with Nikki's temper than become Jonah.

Her fingers released the briefcase handle, letting the heavy object sink into the depths. Instantly Cassidy felt herself able to move more easily and began kicking to the surface. Out of the blue veil straight ahead, her fears manifested themselves. The colossal ocean predator had returned, beginning another attack run.

Shit! Kick faster, Davis!

The megalodon resembled a large, if even bloated, great white shark. Its belly hung down far, as if it had just feasted on an entire blue whale. Its icy eyes pierced through the watery refraction like two great snow-globes, transfixing Cassidy with their glassy brilliance. From its mouth jutted an array of razor-sharp teeth that reminded her of a hungry underwater tyrannosaur. Pushing through the ocean like a naval attack sub, the megalodon quickly went from a blurry shape to perfectly in focus, locking onto the struggling woman.

No!

Cassidy looked one final time at the oncoming megalodon as the giant creature opened its expansive gullet, sucking in bubbles like a carnivorous vacuum. Her heart palpitating quickly as if it would reach a crescendo, the megalodon's mouth expanded until it filled her entire vision – just as she felt Leon's wrinkled hairy hand latch onto hers and haul her from the abyss.

The first thing Cassidy heard over her involuntarily coughing for air was the swell of the wave from the meg's dorsal fin. Her head struck the rough floor of the boat as she felt another wave pass over from the wake, splashing the three others away from the stern. Immediately after the meg's dorsal fin went back under, Nikki's outburst resumed.

"Cassidy, where is it?" came the annoyed voice of the drug kingpin. "Where the hell is my – *our* money?"

Cassidy steadied herself as Leon helped her up.

"Where do you think, bitch?" Cassidy started, coughing up the last of her water. "The damn meg would've swallowed me whole if I didn't drop that clunky thing. Your money is on its way to the bottom of the Pacific.

"*Rauugh!* You stupid *cu* –"

"*Wait!*" Xavier grunted, holding back his employer. "We have a bigger problem right now than the damn drug money."

"You really think I give a damn about that piece-of-shit shark if I'm in this boat?" Nikki said, angrily turning toward Xavier. "No, you asshole! I want that damn money! It's all we could salvage from that bloody rig!"

"I think you'll care a whole lot more about the shark in a little bit if you're floating on the Pacific in just a life vest."

"Xavier, what the hell are *yo*–"

"Nikki, we're sinking!"

"*What?!*"

Nikki stared down at the floor in utter shock and disbelief. Cassidy followed her gaze, grimacing when bubbles frothing in between seams confirmed Xavier's suspicions. It didn't seem to be too disastrous at the moment, but Cassidy knew that once a good portion of the boat had been submerged, the rest would quickly follow.

"What the –"

"The meg must've struck our ship during its last pass," Leon elaborated, eyes bulging in terror as reality was suddenly setting in. "Doesn't look to be too bad, but if we don't figure out a game plan soon, we could be shark-bait. Suddenly, sitting snug on a Coast Guard chopper doesn't seem like such a bad idea."

"I've got an idea," Nikki said, drawing her pistol and aiming it between Cassidy's eyes. "How about I kill you for dropping my money! At least then I'll go to my grave with half a smile on my face."

Cassidy was about to reach for her pistol when Leon stepped between the two women.

"That won't help our current situation," he said. "You shoot her and the blood will mix with the water. If anything, it will only egg the megalodon on to attack with more aggression. We need to do something else."

"How about a flare?" Xavier suggested. "It could be that some good Samaritan comes across and saves us. After we cap them and commandeer their boat, we could be in Cali faster than the blink of an eye. Leave the corpses for the meg. No evidence."

"I'm not talking about flares," Leon said. "Xavier, is that scuba set still on board?"

"Yeah. Why?"

"I'm going down to inspect the propeller," Leon elaborated, stepping into the cabin to retrieve the underwater gear as the others followed. "I spent a few years in the Navy a few years back. Marine Engineering department. Deep sea welding and such. Hell of a business. Anyways, I'm the only one on board who has a chance of figuring it out. It only makes sense if I go."

"You're gonna go into the water with that... that *thing* out there?" Cassidy grimaced. "Leon, please! We can figure out some other *wa* –"

"Quiet, Davis!" Nikki scolded, hair flipping wildly as she turned to Cassidy. "You've already caused enough trouble as it is! Because of you, our only chance of starting the operation up again is gone! You better hope Leon gets this boat going, because that's the only thing keeping me from blowing your damn head off."

"And the money, of course," Leon added, zipping up the wetsuit, "which I may be able to get for you."

"Really?" Nikki exclaimed, her anger melting away to happiness instantaneously.

"Depends on how far down it is," Leon explained, placing goggles over his head. "Maybe we'll get lucky and the case hit a sandbar not far down. I'm stronger than Cassidy. I can haul it up."

"And the propeller?" Xavier asked.

"I won't know until I see it," Leon admitted, stepping out to the rear platform of the stern. "It could be that it's just dislodged somehow. Odds are I may be able to repair it from what I learned in the Navy."

"What about the meg?" Cassidy asked, ignoring Nikki's wrathful gaze.

"It hasn't circled back yet," Leon said. "My guess is it just toyed with us before continuing to the rig wreckage. I can see the smoke from here. There may be enough blood in the water from the battle to lure the meg."

"But how can you be sure?" Cassidy asked.

"We can't," Leon replied. "But if we sit here and do nothing, we'll know soon enough when we're floating in the Pacific. When I'm down there, you three should focus on getting that water out. There're some buckets in the cabin. While two of you are busy throwing the water out, one of you should patch those holes. Supplies should be in the cabinet behind the table. Now wish me luck. We just might make it out of this."

"Good lu –"

Leon jumped backwards off the rear platform, shoving the regulator in his mouth as the ocean swallowed him, leaving Cassidy alone with Nikki and her muscular enforcer. Nikki scowled at her, snapping a finger at the cabin.

"Don't just stand there, bitch," Nikki barked. "Grab a bucket and start sloshing this shit out of here!"

#

Damn this deep water shit, Leon thought as the cold water rushed around him. *I thought I'd seen the end of this line of work.*

Leon Saville had no fear of the ocean. Having shaken off any uncertainties about drowning in his training in the Navy, Leon had come to find solace in his repair work. What he did fear, however, was not being able to hear what was around him. During his tenure with the United States military, Leon could always rely on other deep sea divers to keep watch for sharks and other potential threats lurking about in the deep confines of the world. Now he was alone – or so he hoped.

After the initial dive plunged him ten feet underwater, Leon spun himself in a three-hundred-and-sixty degree angle. He saw a few shapes in the distance that he assumed were dolphins, and a few smaller fish that he couldn't identify.

Thankfully, there was no sign of the megalodon.

First, he decided to inspect the propeller. He swam up to the underside of the boat, aghast by what he saw.

The second pass of the megalodon had conducted damage to the bottom of their craft. Large gashes scuffed the paint from the underside. In sparse areas, pockets of light shined through from the cabin above. Momentarily, shadows would pass in front of the holes blocking the light, which Leon assumed to be Nikki and Xavier trying to conduct damage control from inside. There didn't appear to be any large holes that would be completely unrepairable, but the smaller holes would need to be patched immediately.

Ah, dammit!

The propeller had been completely ripped off from the colossal fish, leaving only a metallic stump behind. Wires hung down freely from the severed component, drifting in the current. Moving the boat via propulsion would be impossible.

That leaves only one objective, Leon surmised, glancing down to the depths. *Retrieving the case. But does it matter if I bring that case to the surface only to find out those assholes can't repair the damage, leaving us to sink anyway? That case could be back down here in no time...*

The area below the boat was encased in a blue veil, telling Leon that they were not anywhere near a sandbar like he had previously hoped. Squinting through his goggles, he was only able to see the writhing forms of a school of fish, but nothing else. Just like salvaging the propeller, recovering the suitcase would be equally impossible.

Nikki's not gonna like this...

A shadow to his left made him stir, forcing the veteran to spin and face the sudden shift in the current.

No! How could I not have seen?

Out from the gloom, a dark shape the size of a small submarine began to contrast itself against the blue water. The megalodon had returned.

Damn!

Leon could feel his teeth struggling to chatter as he bit down on his regulator mouthpiece. He gently began to kick toward the surface, trying not to draw too much attention from the megalodon. Unsure if the shark had directly seen him, Leon continued to kick upward, gaining confidence when the predator started to veer to Leon's left, although still heading for the same direction as the sinking craft.

Leon looked up, confirming how far he still had to ascend before he reached the bow of the boat.

Fifteen feet. Okay, that's doable. Steady, Leo –

In a terrifying turn of events, the megalodon abruptly changed its trajectory, now heading straight for Leon, quickly coming into crystal clear focus.

Hell no! Swim! Swim, you crotchety old bastard!

Leon's docile climb now turned into a desperate scramble for salvation as he kicked and pulled his way skyward. He cast a look back at the meg, confirming that now the gigantic predator had selected him for its next meal. The fish's jaws opened in savory delight as the shark's bulbous head rapidly closed the gap toward Leon's wriggling legs.

How much farther? Five feet! I can see the ladde –

The last thing Leon felt was his teeth breaking apart as his jaw bit down on the regulator, shattering his mandible. A cloud of red water consumed his vision as the metallic glint of the ladder was whisked away. His vision clouded into a blur as his lungs quickly filled with water. As his dying body was hauled away by the primordial predator, Leon died happily knowing one final thought.

At least that bitch won't get her drug money...

4

Cassidy Davis was still on the stern of the boat when Leon's grisly death came to fruition. Trying to hurl water overboard with a bucket, she heard a frothing explosion coming from just over the edge of the watercraft.

Leon! No!

She arrived at the edge of the boat just to see Leon surface – consumed by an explosion of bubbles coated in bloody diluted ocean water. Leon's eyes bulged as his body surfaced, his hands fighting with what lurked below the waves.

Behind the watery red barrier, Cassidy looked on in horror as the megalodon appeared. Primeval teeth crunched down on Leon's ribs, breaking his body nearly in two as the enormous shark swerved away from the stern, hauling the fresh kill back to open water. Cassidy tried to fight off shock as she extended her hand, knowing deep down that her attempt at saving Leon was in vain. In his dying state, Leon extended his hand as well, although a distance of over three feet separated the two shipmates. Then, with an aggressive dive, the megalodon and Leon vanished into the depths. The meg's tail surfaced once as the shark plunged, clarifying the end of the traumatizing encounter.

"*Leon!*" Cassidy cried, clenching the guardrail as she watched the disappearance of the creature.

The sight was something she would never forget. Out of anyone in the drug business that she had grown closest to, almost like a father figure, it had been Leon. The naval veteran had watched her back several times on the oil rig, and the two had formed an unlikely bond. With Leon gone, Cassidy knew it would be just herself with the two murderous cartel members, left to die on a sinking boat – or worse – dying in the water with a hungry predator thought to be extinct for millions of years.

Behind her, she could hear Nikki's clatter of shoes pounding out onto the deck, bearing a look of disapproval and curiosity.

"Where is it, Davis?" Nikki asked with a scowl. "Where's Leon? Does he have the money? What about the propeller? Where the *fu* –"

"The meg took him!" Cassidy cut her off. "It just picked him out of the water and pulled him under! He was taken before he could tell us anything."

"*Dammit!*" Nikki roared, banging a fist against the cabin door frame. "What the hell are we supposed to do if we can't fix that damn propeller? And what about *my* money! It's gone! All because your dumb-ass had to fall overboard still holding the *bloody* suitcase!"

"Don't you understand?" Cassidy fired back. "It doesn't matter if I had your damn money or not! There's a meg out there. If the propeller's out and we can't move, that meg will pick us off one by one when we sink! If dying rich or dying poor are what you're worried about, I promise you, both scenarios will end the same very soon if we can't repair the damage!"

"You stupid *bitc* –"

"*Boss! Boss!*"

Xavier ran through the cabin door, interrupting the conversation. Cassidy froze, seeing Nikki's hand resting on the hilt of her holstered pistol. Cassidy debated going for her own, before she saw her former employer ease off the weapon's hilt.

"What is it, Xavier?" Nikki shrieked. "What could possibly be going wrong now?"

"I can't stop these leaks by myself!" Xavier yelled back, no longer intimidated by the drug lord. "If you two are just gonna bitch at each other up here back and forth, we'll be shark food in minutes. In case you haven't noticed, there's still more holes and the water won't stop flowing!"

The pair of women looked at the floor.

More water had consumed the bottom of the deck, bubbling up through whatever seams that the ocean could find. Just over an inch in depth, Cassidy could feel her shoes fill with water. Every step she took, the water sloshed beneath her feet, making her feel seasick and anxious. Despite the queasy feeling, Cassidy wondered if the damage could still be reversed.

"How many holes still need patching?" Cassidy asked as she resumed throwing water over the side.

"A couple!" Xavier replied swiftly. "Nikki, can you get back to patching them? There're a few obvious ones, but I'm worried about one behind the dashboard console. That's a slow leak, but without tearing apart the whole system, I doubt I'll be able to stop it."

"What about the flare?" Cassidy asked.

"Damn, I forgot all about the flare! We have two shots and –"

"Bullshit are we using that flare!" Nikki roared. "With the Coast Guard probably en route to the rig, they'd be on us in minutes! I'd rather take my chances here or in the water with the meg! The answer is no!"

"You'll change your mind when you're actually *in* the water with the meg!" Xavier replied. "Sorry, Salerno, but we're using the flare – *now!*"

"Not so fast, asshole!" Nikki barked, drawing her pistol.

Xavier froze, staring down the barrel of his ruthless employer's firearm.

"Easy," he said, slowly raising his hands. "Killing me will get you nowhere when you still need me to get this water out. You shoot me – or Davis – and the meg will smell our blood. It will only draw the shark, just like Leon said."

"You touch that flare, and I'll kill you," Nikki said, refusing to back down, a bead of sweat descending her brow.

"Then you'll have to kill me, boss," Xavier said, lowering his hands and beginning to turn to the cabin. "We need help, and the flare is the only way we'll get it. Besides – I'd rather you kill me now than be drowned or ripped apart by the megalodon."

He started back to the cabin, slipping into the door frame. Nikki kept her pistol trained on him as he arrived back on the deck with the orange flare gun. Without hesitating, Xavier lifted the pistol in the air, giving one last look at his disgruntled boss. Nikki locked eyes with him, keeping her pistol trained on his head. Xavier returned the look, refusing to back down.

"Go ahead and do it," he remarked. "'Cause this flare's goin' off."

Nikki gritted her teeth, finger teasing the trigger, but soon gave a long defeated breath. Cassidy was shocked after Nikki lowered her gun, cursing at Xavier's sudden rebellious nature.

"It won't matter," Nikki replied, turning back to the endless ocean. "We're well out of range for those Coast Guard cutters to see us – if there's any that didn't get taken down in the rig shootout."

"I'm praying there are a few," Xavier replied, pulling the trigger.

An orange glowing rocket sailed into the air above the boat. Reaching an altitude of over a hundred feet, the flare exploded, before slowly sinking back down toward them. Cassidy turned back toward the sea, half expecting to see an orange Coast Guard chopper coming to save them.

"Anything?" Nikki asked, staring out through the other side.

"None here," Cassidy replied.

"Good," replied the drug lord. "I didn't want those assholes showing up anyway. Now we can get on with getting this *wat* –"

"There!" Xavier replied, pointing and trembling. "*Meg!* Ten O'clock!"

You gotta be shittin' me! Cassidy thought, fear gripping her as she followed Xavier's finger.

One hundred and fifty yards and closing, the tall dorsal fin had ascended once more from the abyss. The megalodon quickly confirmed its course – a bee-line path directly toward the damaged watercraft.

Cassidy marveled at the speed and precision that the fish showcased, slicing undeterred through the waves like a provoked rhinoceros. At its present speed, the megalodon's assault would be disastrous for their sinking boat.

"*Hang on!*" Xavier called, gripping down on the guardrail. "It's gonna ram us!"

Cassidy turned to Nikki, whose face transitioned into ghostly white. The drug lord's aggressive demeanor had shifted to utter terror. Nikki awkwardly fumbled backward, her back striking the cabin wall next to the door frame. Her jaw dangled open, anticipating a brutal pounding by the meg's colossal head.

"I bet you wish you were snug in a Guard chopper now," Cassidy remarked. Nikki didn't return a look, choosing instead to simply look onward in fright, captivated by the dominant predator.

"Here it comes!" Xavier shrieked, emitting fast breaths that Cassidy judged were the result of a panic attack.

The megalodon's dorsal fin soon towered over them like a small house. Cassidy found herself collapsing to her knees as the shadow of the fin once again dwarfed the boat, flooding them momentarily in eerie darkness. With a powerful surge, another wave crested the boat, flooding the deck with water. Before the trio could recover, the dorsal fin arrived, spinning the ship aggressively to the side before the megalodon vanished under the riptide.

"*Augh!*"

Cassidy was hurled across the deck from the result of the meg's impact. Grunting as she struck the other side of the deck wall, she gripped the guardrail and struggled to her feet – just in time to see Xavier fly past, carried by an aftershock wave. With a barbaric cry, the tattooed enforcer was carried out to the ocean.

"Xavier!" Cassidy yelled, struggling to get to her feet as over a foot of water now filled the deck of the rapidly sinking boat.

Xavier went under, having been carried more than thirty feet out from the boat by the shark's wake. A second later, he surfaced, coughing water aggressively as his tattooed muscular arms fought to keep his body afloat.

"Don't come out after me!" Xavier gagged in between coughs. "It's too dangerous. Just stay in the boa – *auughhh!*"

The ocean around Xavier exploded in a red volcano of blood. Below the surface, the megalodon's jaws appeared, crunching down on the thug's midsection. Blood plagued his white tank-top as Xavier's hands flew down, trying to pry open the shark's jaws like a bear trap to relieve pressure. Cassidy covered her ears as the unbearable sound of bones being shattered cracked over the swell of the ocean roar. Then in one powerful pull, the shark pulled its newest meal down into the depths. Xavier's white tank top was visible for a few more seconds, before vanishing forever into the darkness.

Cassidy struggled to fight back tears, unable to ascertain what she was more startled by – the death of Xavier or knowing she may be the animal's next meal.

Letting go of the guardrail, she looked down. Water from the megalodon's final pass had flooded the upper part of the deck. In certain areas of the floor, she could see bubbling pockets rising more violently between the seams, telling her that the animal's last pass conducted more damage to the hull. The watercraft began to tilt as more ocean water crept up over the stern. Grim reality firmly set in for Cassidy Davis: the boat was more than halfway underwater.

Beside her, Nikki Salerno gripped the deck rail, still awestruck over Xavier's death. Water crept up her leg, leaving her knees as the lowest dry part of her body. Beside Nikki, Cassidy pointed to the ladder leading to the top of the cabin.

"*Climb!*" she ordered.

Nikki promptly obeyed, skin white as a ghost as she realized their getaway vehicle would be under the Pacific in less than a minute. Seconds later, both women were on the top of the cabin, watching in terror as the water completely consumed the deck, creeping up to their last remaining hideout.

The only sign of the megalodon was its last known position, marked by the diluted blood of Xavier that still lingered on the surface. Nikki drew her sidearm, brushing the hair out from her eyes as the drug lord quickly regained her confidence, fueled by a last-minute adrenaline rush.

"That damn shark is gonna have to come and get me!" she cursed, scanning the water with her Beretta. "Davis, why don't you have your gun out?"

"You really think these bullets will stop that thing?" Cassidy replied. "Face it. It's a killing machine, Nikki. It's an apex predator, and if I'm right, it's the largest ocean predator ever known to scientists. We don't stand a chance. You'd be better off using the gun on yourself."

"I always knew you were a coward, Davis," Nikki replied as the water level began to crest the roof, touching the shoes of the two women. "But I never knew you were a quitter."

Nikki turned the pistol toward Cassidy, a devious smile cracking over her pursed lips.

"How about I just kill you first? It's only fair for all the shit you've put me through this last hour."

"You may wanna hold off on that."

"Why's that, bitch?"

"The Coast Guard just showed up."

"*What?*"

Nikki lowered the weapon, turning around to where Cassidy was looking. Just over the horizon, a small-sized Coast Guard Point Class cutter appeared, approaching the sinking drug boat at breakneck speed. Cassidy judged by assessing the boat's position that the military vessel would reach the two women in under a minute.

I hope that's soon enough, Cassidy thought as the water consumed the front of her shoe.

Nikki holstered her weapon. Although her employer tried to hide it, Cassidy noticed a faint smile of relief pass over the drug lord's face.

5

"Get your filthy hands off me, you swine!" Nikki barked as a Coast Guard seaman hauled her onto the cutter. "I didn't think any of you assholes escaped the shootout!"

"Sorry to prove you wrong, Ms. Salerno," replied the soldier as he roughly pulled her onto the cutter after relieving her of her Beretta. "The Coasties are more resilient than you give them credit for."

Another seaman reached for Cassidy's hand. She took it, grateful to be out of the open water, even as the soldier retrieved her sidearm.

She had spent the last fifty seconds in tantalizing suspense as both her and Nikki gradually sunk farther into the ocean. It took only ten seconds for the roof of the cabin to leave their feet, forcing them to tread water until the cutter arrived. Surprisingly, Cassidy realized, the megalodon did not reappear in the time they were floating in the Pacific. She assumed the arrival of the cutter may have deterred the creature, but she didn't rule out the thought that the large predator may still be nearby.

"Thank you," Cassidy replied, taking the soldier's arm by the upper wrist.

She couldn't help but crack a smile as she touched down on the industrial floor of the cutter, fighting back the urge to kiss the ground. The abrupt arrival of loud footfalls shook her from the stupor.

A cleanly shaven man in his mid-forties clad in a white uniform stood in front of the women. As Cassidy stood up straight, she studied the badges and insignia on the man's blazer, immediately identifying him as the man in charge.

"Greetings," the man began. "You may address me as Commander Wilson of the United States Coast Guard. We've been looking for you, Ms. Salerno. If not for that flare, you could've slipped away from our grasp once again. I'm assuming it was your vessel that fired that flare, after all?"

Nikki remained quiet, giving the Coast Guard commander a cold blank stare.

"It was us," Cassidy said, crinkling the bottom of her shirt to wring out the water.

"And who might you be?" Commander Wilson asked, turning his attention to Cassidy.

"Cassidy Davis," she answered. "I'm one of Nikki's associates. We were the ones who fired the flare."

"Are there any other survivors of your cartel left?" Commander Wilson asked, turning back to the drug lord. Nikki again returned his question with an evil glare, ending the stare down by spitting at the commander's feet.

"Charming," Commander Wilson replied, keeping his rigid posture. "It doesn't matter. More helicopters and cutters are inbound. Some naval ships are even joining in the operation. We have most of the exits cut off for miles. If your ship didn't sink when it did, you would've run right into another Coast Guard flotilla. I'll give it to you, Ms. Salerno. Your little devoted army of criminals put up quite the fight at the rig. This showdown will be nationally televised, and will probably be remembered as one of the greatest oceanic battles of our time."

"I'm glad they killed many of your troops!" Nikki snapped. "My only regret is that there wasn't enough time to watch it happen before I bailed out."

"Watch it, Ms. Salerno," replied Commander Wilson. "It's a big ocean out there, and your apprehension hasn't been formally reported yet to the other vessels in the area. Accidents happen from time to time. There are five other troops on this cutter apart from me. None of them would bat an eye if I tossed your ass over. Especially given how your cartel members killed many of their friends."

"You wouldn't dare," Nikki argued. "I'm more valuable alive. I have information on all the other cartels operating from here to Seattle. Keeping me happy is in your best interest, Commander."

"Information can be bought or accrued in other ways," replied Commander Wilson. "I'm sure Ms. Davis here can provide me with all the information we need if something were to happen to you – so if I were you, I'd watch your tone. Now, what happened to your boat? Bullet holes from the shootout? I take it your money is now finding its way to the ocean floor."

"It was a megalodon!" Cassidy butted in. "A megalodon sunk our ship. It killed two of us."

One of the seamen behind the commander laughed, breaking momentarily from his strict military posture as he nearly dropped his submachine gun in laughter.

"Quiet, Hugo!" snapped Commander Wilson, shooting a deliberate glare at the soldier.

"Apologies, sir!" Hugo replied. "It's just such an *absurd* remark."

"I'd have to agree," replied the commander. "Ms. Davis, may I remind you that lying to an officer of the Coast Guard won't get you very far. Now I'm being serious. What happened to your ship?"

"Commander Wilson, I'm telling you what happened," Cassidy said.

"It was either a megalodon or a very large great white shark. It attacked shortly after the shootout on the oil rig. It only passed us a few times – each pass adding more damage to our hull. It didn't take the creature long to sink the craft. Even a ship like this wouldn't be able to take a few direct hits from that shark."

The soldier named Hugo burst out laughing again. This time even Commander Wilson couldn't help but crack a smile.

"Ms. Davis, I think this has gone on long enough," Commander Wilson said, the smile fading from his lips.

"I'm serious, Commander," Cassidy replied. "*Augh*, what it did to Leon and Xavier... I'll never be able to get it out of my head, sir."

"Well hats off to your degenerate friends, Ms. Davis," Commander Wilson said. "But even if there was such a creature out there, it would be no match for a Coast Guard cutter. The weapons on this boat will tear that thing apart. Take a look over there."

Commander Wilson pointed to a large weapon mounted to the front of the boat. The gun was mounted on a swivel platform, bordered on both sides by a white armored barricade for defense.

"That's an Oerlikon 20 millimeter canon," he said, beaming with pride at the sight of the dark weapon. "Capable of firing over three-hundred rounds per minute, this piece of artwork can rip through anything. Sharks are no different. Trust me, you two are safe as can be. And I intend on keeping it that way until I drop both of you off in prison – unless Ms. Salerno keeps mouthing off."

"Those fancy guns didn't help your other Coast Guard buddies," Nikki smirked, egged on by the commander's remark. "Not when our cartel boats picked them off with no problem."

Hugo jumped forward past the commander, drawing a knife to Nikki's throat. He pushed her to the edge of the boat, using his weight to block her escape. The drug lord struggled with the soldier's wrist, but eased up when Hugo pressed the metal blade against her jugular.

"You better quit saying that, bitch!" Hugo grumbled. "Commander Wilson's right. What's stoppin' us from dumpin' your ass into the waves? Maybe you'll even run into that "megalodon". I'd love to see a shark rip you apart for all the shit your cartel has caused the California Guard flotillas."

"Easy, Hugo," Commander Wilson, a hand resting on the soldier's shoulder. "I think Ms. Salerno gets the hint. I think rotting in federal prison will be enough for her –"

"Commander!" a soldier called from the cutter's tower. "Something massive underwater converging on our position. I checked with the other Guard and Navy ships on our scanners. It's nothing in our database. The coordinates indicate it will be on us in under a minute. And it's *big*."

"An attack sub?" Hugo asked, letting Nikki go as the drug lord fought to catch her breath.

"Target surfacing at eleven o'clock!" the soldier in the tower cried over the roar of the engine.

The soldiers and the two fugitives gathered near the cutter's guardrail. Cassidy found herself boxed in from behind by Commander Wilson and Hugo, while bumping shoulders with Nikki. Unable to move, she was forced to watch as her fears once again manifested themselves into reality.

"Holy shit," was all Hugo could manage to say.

Wasting no time in making a grand entrance, the meg's dorsal fin chopped up through the surface, racing toward the cutter, seemingly unimpressed by the naval armament. The shark's caudal fin rose up behind the dorsal, swaying in hypnotic rhythm as the massive carnivore rapidly closed on the ship. Cassidy turned as both Commander Wilson and Hugo suddenly laughed again.

"Well damn," Commander Wilson chuckled. "You were telling the truth after all. Sorry I didn't believe you – well, I suppose I still don't. There's *no* way that's a megalodon. Probably just an overgrown great white. Hell, from this distance it could be a big orca for all I know."

"What kind of orca do you know with a blue fin, dumbass," Nikki uttered, facing the oncoming threat.

"Watch it, Ms. Salerno," Commander Wilson snapped. "Or we just might use you as bait. Hugo, prepare the Oerlikon. Let's show Ms. Salerno and Ms. Davis how we'll turn their mystery fish into canned tuna."

"Aye, sir," Hugo smiled, leaving the trio and walking over to the gunnery port. "This will be good target practice for me. Not that I didn't have enough blowing away half of Salerno's cartel. *Ha-ha-ha!*"

Nikki shot him a cold look as a pair of seamen escorted them back to the base of the cutter's tower. Hugo readied the weapon. Making sure the weapon's safety was off, Hugo swiveled the Oerlikon around, facing the barrel of the machine gun toward the large dorsal fin. Centering the sights to the middle of the fin, Hugo turned back to the commander.

"Fire at will," Commander Wilson smirked.

Hugo nodded, turning back to the sight.

With a maniacal laugh, Hugo unleashed a torrent of gunfire at the shark's dorsal fin. Golden tracer rounds soared from the Oerlikon's barrel as Hugo fought to keep the gun pointed at the target. Most of the rounds missed the fish altogether, but a few shots grazed the fin.

Cassidy squinted through the ocean mist, noticing some blood spurting out from the dorsal fin. Nonetheless, the weapon's firing capabilities were not enough to slow the shark's advance. The megalodon accelerated its approach as the fin began to dip down, closing near Hugo's gunnery platform. Hugo followed the shark's descent with the machine gun's barrel, adjusting the weapon's angle as the fish began to submerge. Cassidy saw Commander Wilson's expression change from confidence to uncertainty, guessing that the soldier now correctly assessed the true size and prowess of the megalodon.

Hugo slowed his firing, mouth dropping in exasperation of trying to control the weapon. The megalodon plunged beneath the side of the cutter, having arrived at its next potential feeding ground. Cassidy gripped a rail mounted against the cutter's tower, anticipating another sonic boom from the shark's dominant weight. In the turmoil, she saw Nikki doing the same.

"*Ah!*" Cassidy cried as the impact rocked the cutter.

The boat listed to its side as a small amount of water passed over the deck. Cassidy felt Commander Wilson and the pair of soldiers tumble to the floor, unprepared for the shark's brutal collision with the cutter. Nikki remained upright opposite Cassidy, grabbing another rail. A piercing scream cut through the air as the firing of the machine gun ceased.

Hugo was airborne, having been shot into the air like a catapult when the megalodon struck the side of the boat. Flying ten feet into the air as the cutter veered to the side, the seaman was powerless to grab hold of the edge railing, instead falling down to the waves below. Cassidy watched helplessly as the seaman vanished over the side, arms and legs flailing in an attempt to reach for the guardrail.

"Man overboard!" Commander Wilson bellowed, racing for the edge. "Someone, throw him a –"

"*AUGHHHH!*"

Before anyone could arrive to throw Hugo a life-vest, the megalodon had circled back, latching onto the seaman's torso. Breaking the soldier's rib cage, the shark pulled its newest meal under the waves. Water raced down the man's throat before he was able to scream. Cassidy arrived at the guardrail just in time to see the corpse fading away under the murky surface.

"*Dammit!*" Commander Wilson cursed. "He's gone! That shark took him! That... that *megalodon* just took him."

"Sir!" called the soldier in the tower, whom Cassidy assumed was driving the boat. "Damage to the hull! Whatever hit us, we're taking on water down below!"

"Well then get to it!" Commander Wilson yelled back. "If we sink, that monster will –"

Gunshots rang out through the deck. Blinded by a muzzle flash, Cassidy dropped to her knees, rolling away from the oncoming fire. Commander Wilson did the same, scrambling away in the other direction.

What the hell? Cassidy thought, finally finding cover behind an industrial ventilation pipe. Cautiously she gained the courage to look over to see what transpired.

In the confusion, Nikki had grabbed one of the seamen's submachine guns. The soldier was lying dead on the ground while the drug lord quickly popped another clip into the weapon. The remaining soldier on the deck – the other one tasked with guarding the drug lord – dove for cover around the other end of the tower, returning fire as he ducked into safety.

"Rot in hell, you assholes!" Nikki laughed uncontrollably, sending another barrage of gunfire recklessly all over the deck. "This isn't the end – do you hear me! I'll rebuild the *entire* cartel piece by piece until we're all over the West Coast!"

How could this get any worse?

Over the drug lord's angry tirade, the familiar splashing of water was heard over the deck. Cassidy turned, just in time to see the megalodon's powerful dorsal and caudal fins surface, before the creature began its powerful charge once more.

Oh... that's how.

6

Bullets tore across the deck in all directions as Nikki unloaded on Commander Wilson's hiding place. Cassidy covered her ears as the commander drew his firearm from the other side of the deck, firing back at the drug lord with a Sig Sauer pistol. The other soldier on the deck tried to fire back at Nikki from his position, but the drug lord ducked into a doorway, avoiding the hailstorm. Shouts from guards up in the tower trickled through the weapons fire exchange as the rest of the ship became aware of the shootout. An alarm began to blare, adding to the volatile conflict.

Nikki, you're one crazy bitch!

Cassidy took one last look at the oncoming megalodon fin, knowing that the Coast Guard cutter would soon suffer the same fate as the speedboat. As she scrambled for cover, she decided that her best bet was to figure out how to disengage the cutter's escape speedboat from the stern and make for the California coast.

Too bad I'm not a damn Coast Guard seaman, Cassidy thought. *Maybe Commander Wilson will –*

"Luke, concentrate your fire at her!" the commander yelled, moving up from his cover. "Keep her pinned! I might be able to get off a clear shot!"

"Aye sir –"

The seaman named Luke caught a bullet to the skull from Nikki's submachine gun. Blood splattered out from the soldier's forehead while momentum pushed his body backwards. Cassidy cringed as the cadaver slipped off the side of the cutter, followed by a loud splash when the body struck the Pacific.

"*No!*" Commander Wilson screamed, standing up as he popped off rounds at Nikki's position. Nikki returned fire before ducking back into the doorway, tracer rounds whizzing past her hair. From over her cover, Cassidy watched as Nikki fled further into the entrance to the tower, running down an industrial corridor. Taking the fight to his antagonist, Commander Wilson followed her into the tower, where the gunfire exchange commenced.

"How do I figure this damn thing out?" Cassidy mumbled as she ran for the escape boat.

Frantically she pushed and pressed through the complex web of releases and control mechanisms, failing to free the small escape speedboat from the stern.

"Come on, *dammit!*"

Over the roar of gunfire from somewhere inside the tower, Cassidy desperately tried to decipher how the Coast Guard cutter's controls worked. She remembered several times back on the oil rig how Leon had tried to teach her simple boating procedures like freeing a boat from a release station. Each time she disregarded his teachings, finding them boring or thinking she would never have to put them into practice. It was a decision she had come to regret.

Finally, she stood up, anxiously kicking the operation panel in distress.

"Come on, you son of a *bit –*"

The sound of the ocean swelling interrupted her outburst.

In her efforts to escape the doomed cutter, Cassidy failed to remember the megalodon was charging the vessel. As the dorsal fin towered above her, the shark struck the side of the cutter before vanishing beneath, undoubtedly causing the hull more damage and increasing the flooding somewhere below.

"*Aughh!*"

The megalodon's impact sent her the way of Hugo – airborne and headed for the edge of the boat. The world around her became an entangled mess of blue blurs, her eyes struggling to make sense of the endless ocean and sky. A knot began to well up in her stomach, but staving off the nausea would have to wait.

Somersaulting mid-air with her face staring at the chaotic swell below, Cassidy outstretched her arms as far as she could as the guardrail slid beneath her. In an instant she felt her palms enclose around the rusty rail. Swinging around like an Olympic gymnast, her body struck the side of the cutter as her hands struggled to hang on.

"Awh!" she winced as a small trickle of blood dripped down her forehead from the impact against the metal siding.

Is the meg still beneath me? Oh shit! I can't stay here. Must climb! Yes, climb now!

"*Help!*" she cried, swinging her feet wildly as she tried to climb back up. Using her shoes and knees, Cassidy tried to push back to the deck, only for gravity to suck her back down. One of her hands let go of the rail as her body swung sideways, adding pressure to her wrist like a twisting rope.

"Ah, *no!*" she cried under the strain.

The words slipped her lips as the great shark passed beneath her. Buried some fifty feet under the water, she could make out the meg's gargantuan shape, stretching to a length of over twenty meters. Headed back out to open water for another pass, Cassidy watched as the megalodon's knife-like dorsal fin ascended back to the surface.

Finally, inertia swung her back around to the wall of the boat, ending her view of the aquatic nightmare.

Have to move! If it comes back for another hit, the damn shark will send me to the Pacific.

Over the edge, she heard the continued rattle of gunfire, followed by human cries as bullets found their fateful targets.

Hopefully there's at least one person left alive that knows how to operate the damn escape boat!

Throwing her palm upward, Cassidy breathed a relieving sigh as her other hand grabbed the rail. Her shoe found an indent in the side of the boat, giving her the leverage she needed to get one elbow over the top. Adrenaline pumping in, she hauled the rest of her fatigued body over the top – just as the megalodon's massive mouth snapped beneath her.

"YAAHHH!"

The shark's mouth closed five feet below her shoe, letting off a loud chomp as the fish's body rammed into the boat's starboard side.

"Oof!"

Pain rippled up her back as her spine struck the adjacent deck wall; the creature's hit having propelled her to the complete opposite side of the ship. Blurry flashes and water molecules obscured her vision momentarily. She laid there for a moment, until her vision came into focus, narrowing on a small trickle of water bubbling up from an air vent on the cutter's deck.

Son of a bitch has already done enough damage to the boat to let it sink!

"I'm not dyin' here today," she groaned. "Not yet. Not without a fight."

She steadied herself, using the cutter's perimeter guardrail. By now, the megalodon would be beginning another attack run. With each hit, more damage would be tallied to the hull, adding to her urgency to escape.

The deck looked very different than it had since she had been nearly tossed into the ocean. Nikki's disastrous firefight had resulted in several blazing fires among the floor, climbing up various pipes and storage crates. The relentless attack from the megalodon manifested in a crooked tilt on the deck, sending most of the residual water collecting in a pool on the opposite side. Somewhere below, she could hear the rush of water as the ocean quickly flooded a chamber, sparking industrial ports and computerized driving mechanisms.

"Come on, Cass! Think. You need to find a way to deploy the speedboat. Find Commander Wilson and tell him the ship is lost! If he's

still alive. Dammit, you should've told him the truth! You should've told him the whole truth the moment you stepped on this ship!

Since her falling over the edge, she came to realize the gunfire inside had suddenly ceased.

Is everyone on the ship dead?

She staggered forward, her shoes touching down on a thin layer of water as she made her way across the deck, reminding her of the final moments spent on the sinking speedboat. Objects began moving down the floor as the cutter continued to tilt at an odd angle, gravity sucking them toward the low point. One of the objects Cassidy quickly recognized, grabbing it as it slid past.

Luke's gun!

She picked up the weapon, checking the magazine. The weapon had about half a clip left.

"Better than nothin'," she muttered, jamming the cartridge back into the firearm as she made her way toward the entrance to the tower.

The hallway inside was consumed with exhaust shooting out from bullet-riddled pipes, making Cassidy gag as she walked discreetly through the hissing vapor. Her only hope to escape was to locate someone who knew how to operate and detach the escape boat. But would the watercraft be enough to outrun the primordial fish that lurked somewhere beneath the sinking cutter?

I'm countin' on it...

The first thing Cassidy saw as she exited the cloud of pressurized exhaust was the cadaver of a seaman. A bullet found its way into the unfortunate man's skull, rendering the poor soldier a crumpled corpse against the industrial wall. She recognized him as the man who first alerted Commander Wilson that the megalodon was coming.

Sorry, pal.

Keeping the machine gun aimed ahead of her, Cassidy followed the corridor as it swung in a one-hundred-and-eighty degree arc, leading up a small stairwell to the control room of the tower. Two more bodies of additional seamen were strewn about on the stairs, ripped apart by gunfire.

Suddenly, another impact from the megalodon rocked the cutter, ramming Cassidy against the corridor wall. Above, the lights flickered once, sparking in their glass encasement before flooding the hall in darkness. Below in the hull, more water could be heard surging into the bowels of the ship, increasing the strain on the fragile structure. The ship began to groan under the increased pressure as Cassidy turned to the stairwell.

It won't be long now...

Splashing out from the inch deep water that glazed over the lower floor, Cassidy made her way up the stairs past the two bodies, carefully avoiding the cascading waterfall of blood. Finally she made her way to the tower control room, greeted by a shocking scenario.

"I'll do it!" came an angry female voice, loud enough to be heard over the blaring alarm. "I'll do it – I *swear!*"

"Go ahead and do it! I'll be dammed before I tell you anything about how to escape!"

Nikki Salerno had a gun aimed at Commander Wilson's head. Standing in front of a control room riddled with bullets that malfunctioned the cutter's capabilities, the drug lord made the commander get down on his knees, preparing to execute the killing shot. In her eyes she bore a look of hatred, keeping her gun trained on the surrendered officer's head as she savored the moment.

"If you don't tell me how to operate that escape boat," Nikki muttered, "then I have no reason to keep you alive, Commander. Soon, you'll join all your dead comrades."

"Put the gun down, Nikki," Cassidy ordered, walking into the small control room, aiming the submachine gun at her former employer.

"*Augh*, Davis. You're such a boy scout! I thought you fell overboard!"

"I can't let you kill him, Nikki."

"He's scum, Davis. He threatened to throw us to the meg!"

"Just you, bitch," replied Commander Wilson, staring up defiantly at the drug lord. His courage earned him a swift strike to the face from the butt of Nikki's pistol. The commander shrieked and crumpled to the floor, before rising back to his kneeling position, continuing to look death defiantly in the eye.

"You can go ahead and kill me," continued the hostage. "If you think I'll tell you anything about how to escape, you're even *crazier* than I thought you were! Have fun on your trip to the bottom of the Pacific. I think your big friend down there will be pleased to meet you."

"You crazy old bastard," Nikki said with a scowl, gritting her teeth. "I swear, I'll do it! I'll do it if you don't tell me how to work the damn boat!"

"No you won't," Cassidy replied, stepping into the room. "I have a clean shot on you, Nikki. I've seen you do horrible, terrible things to your own kind on the rig. I've wanted to stop you for so long. And now, that time has finally come."

"You couldn't hit the broad side of a Santa Monica home, Davis," Nikki laughed. "I've seen your shootin'. Hell, today you didn't hit any of the other Coast Guard seamen in the rig shootout."

"Are you really that naive, Nikki?" Cassidy smiled. "After all this time, I was worried that you would've actually caught on. There was a reason that I didn't shoot any of the others..."

"What are you talkin' about, bitch?"

"I've been working undercover with the DEA for six years," Cassidy smiled. "We've been monitoring your cartel's progress, using your operation for intel on the other cartels that have been popping up along the West Coast in the past decade. When I knew we'd harvested all the information out of you that we could, we decided to pull the plug on your cartel. Before long, we'll be going after all the others as well."

Nikki scowled, her hand trembling as she shook the gun. Commander Wilson's mouth hung agape, blown away by the startling discovery.

"Who do you think called the Coast Guard about your whereabouts?" Cassidy winked. "I led them right to your front door, bitch."

7

"You conniving little bitch!" Nikki roared, her hand continuing to shake as she kept the gun aimed at Commander Wilson. "I knew it! I knew there was something *off* about you. No one that's ever worked for my cartel has been that terrible of a shot. And it wasn't the first time either – you refused to execute some of the workers who tried to short me of cash! I had to make Xavier finish the job! *Gaugh!* I should've added you to the execution list for your insubordination!"

"You should have," Cassidy smiled calmly.

"How did the screening process miss you?" Nikki asked coldly.

"I was brought in by Rob Peters," Cassidy replied, "Who as you may or may not know, vouched for me to get in. After he left your cartel, he did time for a double homicide in downtown LA. We got to him there and managed to conjure up a deal where his sentence was reduced if he talked me up to his cartel connections – *your* cartel. After that, I had a meeting with Xavier, and the rest took care of itself. I don't think your enforcer ever came to suspect anything either, if it makes you feel better."

Cassidy could sense Nikki's blood boiling as her hand trembled. The DEA agent kept her machine gun aimed at the drug lord's head. In the background, the bow of the boat began to rise slowly into the air, reminding her of the famous Titanic incident.

We must be taking on more water below, Cassidy surmised. *I can't stay here much longer...*

"So... what happens now, Agent Davis?" Nikki scowled.

"What happens now is that you put the gun down and I take you in to one of the other Coast Guard boats. Sorry I didn't tell you about myself earlier, Commander Wilson. I was a little shook up from the encounter with the megalodon."

"Apology accepted," Commander Wilson replied. "But I have a better idea. Why not kill her and the two of us can make for one of the nearby cutters in our detachable speedboat?"

"*What?*" Cassidy asked, shocked by the officer's callous statement.

"Before the shootout, I had my men send out a distress call. By now, several cutters in the vicinity are en route to pick us up – provided the megalodon doesn't get to us first. Ms. Salerno here has proven too dangerous to be taken in alive. I don't have any handcuffs on board, so there's no way to detain her. If she somehow gets the upper hand if we try to take her out in the escape boat, do you really think she'll spare our lives? She could kill us both and dump us overboard, letting our blood attract the shark so she can get away. And from the way I take it, the two of you haven't had the best working relationship. She'll kill you as soon as she finds the opportunity, Agent Davis."

"He's right, Agent Davis," Nikki smiled. "It would be a pleasure – doing something I should've done a *long* time ago..."

"I'm not a murderer, Commander," Cassidy replied, shooting the officer a stern look. "You expect me to ignore months of training and preparation for this sting operation, just to execute the main objective that the DEA wants to apprehend?"

"You'd be doing us all a favor," Commander Wilson replied. "You and I both know how many people the Salerno Cartel has killed over the years. They've killed many of my comrades, as I'm sure they've also killed people from the DEA and other agencies that got in their way. If she kills us and gets away, then this nightmare will start all over again. Ms. Salerno has great influence in the criminal underworld. Do you really want to take that chance?"

"He's right, Agent Davis," Nikki smiled. "Do you?"

"Be quiet, Nikki!" Cassidy snapped. "I'm not about to kill you, but I may just pop you one in the leg to make matters easier!"

"I'd leak blood all the way to the next cutter," Nikki laughed. "And our friend the megalodon will surely follow. You'd be better off shooting me..."

"Nikki! I said be *quiet!* Commander, we can both take her in. We'll just put her in the front of the boat. We'll both have guns – it'll be a piece of *cak* –"

A gunshot rang out through the cutter's control room as Commander Wilson's skull splattered open. Blinded temporarily by the sudden muzzle flash, Cassidy watched as blood spurted out from the back of the officer's head, coating a control panel in a crimson sheen. The uniformed cadaver slumped down on the metal floor, clanging loudly as the commander's forehead struck the rivets. Nikki started to turn her weapon toward her remaining opponent, but Cassidy was already eyeing her.

"Put it down, Nikki," Cassidy barked, blinking blood from her eyes. "My orders were to take you alive, but if you turn your weapon on me, then you give me no choice..."

Nikki smiled devilishly, dropping her machine gun to the floor.

"Good luck getting out of here, Agent Davis. I've killed the last man alive who knew anything about disengaging that escape boat – if the stern is still above water, that is..."

"Looks like we're both going down together then," Cassidy replied.

"I think not," Nikki said, entranced by something out the window. "What are *you* –"

A familiar impact rocked the starboard side of the cutter, pushing the tower over at nearly a forty-five degree angle. Cassidy felt her feet leave the ground, launched into the air once again by the megalodon's thunderous impact. To her front, Nikki's body was hurled against the side wall of the tower. Shattering the protective glass, the drug lord's form flew off the tower, landing with a thud somewhere on the deck below.

"*Augh!*" Cassidy cried as she saw stars, knowing that her head had struck the ceiling of the tower control room. Her palms felt the cold tingle of riveted metal as she braced herself for the rough landing. Turning her head, she came face to face with the frozen expression of the ruthless Commander Wilson as he lay static on the floor.

I can't take much more of this...

The gleam of metal caught her eye from the corner of the room, and a second later Luke's gun was back in her hand. As she regained her footing, through the broken glass of the tower's windows, the familiar sight of the megalodon's dorsal fin drifted past, before submerging again into the Pacific.

Son of a bitch just won't let us live, will it?

A sudden swelling of ocean made her spin around. A torrent of bubbling water exploded into the lower hallway from under the hall, quickly rising up the stairs as it threatened to consume the first of the Coast Guard seaman cadavers. In the conduit above, the alarm sparked, ceasing the incessant blaring.

It's going down fast!

The corridor compromised, Cassidy turned her attention to the broken glass from whence Nikki's body was tossed out of. She approached the edge and looked down. Below, the ocean had not managed to envelop the rapidly sinking cutter, although trickles of waves were beginning to roll over the side. The crackle of extinguishing fires hissed as repercussion effects from the firefight met their match against the megalodon's attacks. Lastly, Cassidy noticed that Nikki's body was nowhere in sight.

Why do I have the feeling that I haven't seen the last of her?

Cassidy shrugged the thought aside, letting herself accept the free fall of the fifteen foot plunge until her body struck the metal floor below. The chill of the sea mist lapped against her face, and she remembered the objective at hand: capture Nikki and escape!

Okay, bitch. Where are you?

Gun in hand, Cassidy veered around, walking cautiously along the side of the boat to the rear platform. Several residual fires still burned along the various ports and junction boxes, only to be extinguished with a sudden wave. The chill of ocean water splashed roughly over her face as the cutter continued its inevitable tilt. Gravity forcing her to hug the wall of the tower, Cassidy followed the pathway around until she made it to the half-sunken stern of the boat, greeted by a familiar foe.

Amid the rapidly filling deck, Nikki Salerno was at the escape boat, quickly pressing through the controls. Screaming as part of the console sparked in response to water intake, Nikki shielded her eyes and jumped back, taking note that she was being watched.

Cassidy readied her weapon in response, anticipating a volatile showdown with her rival.

Marveling at the speed at which the drug dealer swiveled her hand around, Nikki toted the gun in the DEA agent's direction.

"See you in *hell*, Agent Davis!" laughed the criminal as she let fly a carefree volley of chaotic rounds.

Cassidy returned fire, running along the deck as she took cover behind a large pipe. As the bullets transitioned into little fireworks as they struck the side of the tower, Cassidy found time to reload, watching as a steady stream of water flew out from the tower entrance, adding strain to the already sinking stern.

Nikki took cover behind the escape boat, swapping out magazines before sending another stream of bullets in Cassidy's direction.

"*Ha!* I've done it!" came the drug lord's wicked voice. "I've figured out this dammed control rig!"

To her horror, the agent heard the detachment process beginning. Gaining courage to glance over her cover, she saw that the boat was now floating on the flooded deck. Somehow, against all odds, Nikki Salerno had managed to decipher the Coast Guards depleted console controls, releasing the evacuation craft.

"What are you gonna do, Agent Davis?" Nikki laughed, wading through the waist deep sunken deck. "You shoot at me, and you risk hitting the escape boat. It's no worry though, since *I'll* be the one taking it! *Ha-ha-ha!*"

Cassidy tried to engage, only to retreat back as another burst from Nikki's submachine gun fire sailed toward her, sending sparking showers over her cover. When she was finally able to return fire, she aimed poorly and high, heeding Nikki's warning to avoid hitting the small escape watercraft. From behind her barricade, she heard the drug lord grunt as she clumsily rolled into the boat.

After taking careful aim, Cassidy heard a defeating click – her weapon was spent of ammunition, and she didn't have a spare cartridge to resume the firefight.

"It's over, Davis!" Nikki yelled, turning to start the boat's motor.

Cassidy ducked down, weighing her options, none of which looked attractive. It was either die from gunfire, die from drowning, or die from the megalodon. Out of those three options, she figured her odds were still the best against Nikki Salerno.

It's now or never, Davis. You have to do this – or you'll be stranded here on a sinking cutter with a hungry megalodon floating nearby.

She looked up again, confirming her enemy was still busy trying to start the motor.

Cassidy capitalized on her opponent's distraction, running toward the floating craft. Nikki heard her coming as she thudded across the deck and turned to fire. A maniacal smile cracked across the drug lord's face as the DEA agent arrived within firing range – only to realize at that critical moment that her weapon had jammed.

"*Dammit!* Stupid Coast Guard *gu –*"

Using the unsunken part of the deck to her advantage, Cassidy bolted across the soaked floor, jumping into the air the moment the water line began. Her jump earned her enough momentum to fly over the small body of water – directly into Nikki's escape boat. The drug lord stared at the agent in shock as her weapon failed to fire. Cassidy extended her right leg, preparing for a move she hadn't executed since her basic combat training for the Drug Enforcement Agency.

"Oh, shit – *ooof!*"

Feeling the brunt of Cassidy's momentum in the form of an outstretched shoe heel to her abdomen, Nikki grunted in agony. Her sub machine gun clattered onto the boat's floor as the drug lord was kicked off the craft, flying into the ocean with a loud splash.

Okay, Davis – think! How do you work this thing?

Quickly calculating how to operate the escape boat's motor and driving functions, Cassidy guided the boat out past the deck, feeling the ship's fragile hull bump once against the cutter's sunken guardrail, before continuing out to open water. Nikki surfaced a second later, coughing up water as she cleared her lungs, clawing at the surface.

"Davis, please don't leave me! I promise! I'll be good. Don't leave me out here with that *thing!*"

"Hang on, Nikki," Cassidy replied, turning the boat's wheel as she guided it closer to Nikki's position.

"Oh, *God!* Davis – I think it's *coming!* Hurry!"

Even before Nikki could continue, Cassidy took note of the large behemoth shadow that materialized under the water. The shadow soon transitioned to the sinister shape of the megalodon's large head. Opening its jaws wide, revealing rows of serrated teeth, the shark positioned its gullet directly under the drug lord's position. Then with an impressive surge, the megalodon burst up from underneath her, engulfing the cartel queen whole in a massive gulp. Nikki had no time to scream – the megalodon's mouth slammed shut after its meal slid down its throat, severing one of the woman's hands by the wrist.

"Augh!"

Cassidy fell over in the boat as the shark's sudden hurtle out of water sent a violent wave at her, knocking the escape boat farther away from the doomed cutter. She looked up just in time to see the megalodon's massive body flying over her boat. Finally, the caudal fin passed overhead as the shark executed a perfect dive back into the ocean on the adjacent side of the boat, ending with another dizzying splash that thrust her boat in a nauseating spin.

As the caudal gin disappeared back into the abyss, Cassidy shuddered at one simple thought.She was alone.

8

With the bubbles diminishing in the wake of the megalodon's plunge, Cassidy turned back to the boat's wheel. She glanced over the dashboard, grateful that the firefight didn't damage any of the vehicle's controls or gauges. Her hand clenched the cold steel of the throttle, easing the boat away from the sinking debris field.

The once pristine Coast Guard cutter headed by Commander Wilson was nearly underwater. Waves completely flooded the deck as water from below streamed through the entrance to the tower. Flames from Nikki's reckless firefight crept off the side of the tower, created from burned out barrels that had since been extinguished by the rising waters.

Cassidy took one last look at the rippling surface where the megalodon vanished, half expecting Nikki to somehow escape the shark's clutches, like she had accomplished many times to evade capture by the military. Finally, Cassidy continued to push the throttle forward, leaving the site of the wreckage.

If the meg's bite force didn't kill her instantly, the shark's rapid descent into heavier water pressure would've...

Roaring away from the besieged craft, Cassidy gunned the engine, giving a final glance back. The ocean crawled over the remaining fragments of the cutter's deck and quickly rose up to consume the bulk of the tower. Seconds later, the top of the tower bubbled into the Pacific, leaving no trace of the treachery of the megalodon. Turning back to the wheel, Cassidy accelerated, eager to leave the ship's resting place behind.

Okay, Wilson said something about more cutters inbound – hopefully I run into one soon...

The dashboard below revealed the boat's motor functions and internal computer were working accurately. The compass bore a heading of East – the direction of the California shoreline. Cassidy smiled.

Maybe this nightmare will all be behind me.

An explosion of ocean fifty yards ahead quickly shook off her positive outlook.

"*AUGH! No!*"

The resurgence of the megalodon confirmed a theory that Cassidy had been speculating upon – the shark had no intentions of leaving anyone from the sting operation alive. She guessed that the animal's salacious appetite had been created by its recent mass consumption of human food. Much blood had been spilled in the water around the rig, possibly drawing the behemoth from the depths of the ocean. The combination of human blood and the creature's instincts to hunt created a lust for slaughter in the primordial shark – a lust it yearned to satisfy.

The thing's not gonna stop until I'm dead!

Gaining confidence in its innate ability to conduct diving attacks, the megalodon rose above the escape boat like an aquatic manifestation of the grim reaper. Even though the creature was of immense weight, the megalodon's momentum earned an altitude higher than that of the boat, which would grant the carnivore an opportunity to devour its target whole. Cassidy took note of the shark's large teeth, watching as they jutted through the gums like arrowheads. The animal's mouth opened wide to receive her, exposing the dark chasm of the meg's gullet.

"Whoa!"

Reflexes kicking in as reality sped up, Cassidy swung the boat to the left, arcing the craft in a near ninety degree angle. Groaning under pressure, the boat complied and executed the swift turn with seconds to spare. The megalodon flew past like an out-of-control Mack truck, twisting its head sideways as it attempted to pluck Cassidy from the vessel. The maneuver failed, and the great predator vanished back into the ocean with a colossal splash.

Can I outrun it? Cassidy thought, her heart thumping quickly.

The thought was plausible, she was sure, when dealing with a normal predator like an average-sized great white shark. But against something the size of a small building, Cassidy had doubts that the boat could outrun a mature megalodon.

A quick glance back told her the predator was about to begin another attack run. She saw the massive dorsal and caudal fins surface as the animal headed for the direction of the sunken cutter, before beginning a graceful turn back around to her direction, restarting the chase. The shark's turn allotted Cassidy time to gain speed as she flew toward the presumed shoreline of California.

The time advantage didn't last for long however – the submerged megalodon accelerated to a rate that initially rivaled that of her boat, but soon was gaining ground on the fleeing watercraft. Cassidy watched in horror as the dorsal fin grew closer and closer, the sounds of its approach rivaling the sound of the engine.

Come on! Go faster, you militarized hunk-of-junk! If that thing attempts another flying attack, it could crush me!

Suddenly, she heard a faint whirring over the shark's colossal fins as they pulverized waves generated by her propeller. On the horizon ahead, an orange speck appeared in the sky, gradually growing larger as it approached her position.

A Coast Guard Jayhawk Chopper!

Cassidy looked over her shoulder at the megalodon's massive dorsal fin, then back at the military helicopter.

They have to see it... They have to see what's following me. But just in case it doesn't register to them that I need help...

She reached down on the dashboard panel where a flare gun had been strapped to a shelf beside the throttle controls. Unstrapping the pistol, she aimed the orange flare gun toward the sky and pressed the trigger, sending a hot spark soaring into the air where it exploded several hundred yards ahead of the helicopter. Cassidy smiled when the helicopter began to descend in altitude, realizing the pilots must have got the hint.

The megalodon continued its inevitable advance, wriggling back and forth in a seamless pattern below the surface as Cassidy tried in vain to zigzag. Twisting and throwing the boat back and forth, she grimaced as the shark kept on her like a computerized tracking missile. Throwing the megalodon off her trail by way of maneuver was pointless, and if the shark had sunken larger ships, it could sink her fledgling little escape craft with ease

The only hope is the chopper!

As she fixed her eyes on the coming salvation on the horizon, she heard a loud swell behind her. Jerking the wheel to the right as a reflex, Cassidy turned – horrified as she was staring at an airborne megalodon with its jaws fully opened, revealing its dark gullet once more.

"*Augh!* Get away from me, you *bitch!*"

The move was enough to carry her out of harm's way by means of the shark's hungry appetite, but it wasn't enough to avoid the shark entirely. Flying past her head, the shark's right collided with the edge of Cassidy's boat, splintering and fracturing the structure. Dozens of geysers shot up from the floor as the megalodon descended back into the sea.

"*SHIT!*"

She looked down in utter shock at what had happened. The right side of her small boat had been completely eviscerated in the creature's pounce. Water quickly began to filter through the gaps, forming a solid puddle that consumed the floor of the boat. The vessel had stopped moving, consuming enough water that the propeller could no longer push the craft forward. Cassidy swallowed hard, knowing the boat would be under the ocean in less than a minute.

I guess it's all up to the helicopter now...

Hastily throwing on a life vest that she found in the storage compartment under the wheel, Cassidy clambered up to the bow of the craft as the stern began to fill with water. Just as it had been with the Coast Guard cutter, the bow began to lift upward, buying her only additional seconds of safety as the stern plunged beneath the waves.

She scanned the immediate vicinity for the next appearance of the dreaded dorsal fin, but the megalodon had yet to surface.

Son of a bitch is toying with me, Cassidy thought as she watched the water quickly rise up to the bow.

The whirring of the helicopter blades grew to a deafening crescendo as she looked upwards. The chopper was still a hundred yards away, but was beginning to arrive within ten feet above sea level. From the side of the aerial vehicle, she could see a door opening and a uniformed crewman waving at her.

Come on, dammit!

Suddenly she could feel the water creeping up to the tip of her shoes... her ankle... her knees...

With a subtle jump, she hopped off the sunken bow, feeling the vehicle leave her body and begin its descent down to the ocean floor beneath. Trying not to make too much commotion as she waded around the surface, she stared out anxiously, gulping as she soon pinpointed the location of the meg.

As if trying to time its next attack with the arrival of the helicopter, the megalodon surfaced a hundred yards away, turned back toward the last known point of the vehicle, then rapidly shot towards her, quickly gaining speed.

Oh no, Cassidy swallowed as she paddled on the surface. *This is it...*

Over the swell of the ocean and the meg's swift approach, she heard a sudden *crack,* followed by several others.

Huh? she thought, the sound reminding her of a baseball connecting with a wooden bat.

The Jayhawk had its side door open. A soldier clad in Coast Guard aviation attire was standing in the opening, firing a shotgun with incendiary rounds. Each round struck the fin, making the megalodon flinch in pain. By the time the fourth round struck the meg's rubbery exterior, a flame managed to catch along the top of the fin.

Cassidy watched in utter shock as the megalodon abandoned the charge, diving back below the ocean only feet in front of her to extinguish the flame.

"Augh!" she winced as the wave from the megalodon's wake pushed her under.

By the time she surfaced, she gripped a Coast Guard harness that had been tossed down to her. For the first time in the day, as she latched the harness around her body, she felt safe.

The Jayhawk was hovering only twenty feet above, creating concentric waves with its turbulent blades. The seaman in the chopper's opening looked down at her from his black visor, waving a thumbs up to confirm that she had secured it around her. When Cassidy returned the wave, she felt herself beginning to be pulled up.

Thank God! I've made it! I'm getting out of this nightmare!

Gaining altitude rapidly, the Jayhawk began an ascent back to the skies. Cassidy felt her waist leave the ocean, followed by her thighs and shoes as the chopper hauled her skyward.

Thank God! It's over... it's over...

Cassidy felt her heart rate decreasing, her muscles relaxing. She could see the man above pulling her closer to the helicopter as the clouds grew closer. Suddenly the man stopped, backing into the helicopter in shock – that's when Cassidy heard the loud swell of the ocean growing beneath her.

Turning her head downward and witnessing something that she knew would haunt her nightmares for years to come, she came face to face with an airborne megalodon, watching helplessly as the colossal carnivore launched itself out of the ocean like a volcanic explosion. The animal grew closer and closer, its caudal fin leaving the surface of the ocean as its entire bulk hovered over the waves. Cassidy lost her breath as her skin turned cold, watching as the rows of razor-sharp teeth stretched wide toward her. In the shark's eyes spun the cyclic blades of the Jayhawk, threatening to rob her of salvation in that horrific moment.

"OoO-ph!"

Somewhere above, the pilot jerked the chopper skyward, hauling Cassidy out of the way of the megalodon as the shark fell backwards. Forced to watch as the ocean shrunk beneath her, she witnessed the megalodon crash back into the waves, consumed by the ocean once more as the helicopter attained a safe altitude that the predator would never achieve.

Unable to look away from the sea of water far below, Cassidy suddenly heard a voice.

"Are you okay, Agent Davis?" asked the soldier as he helped her into the Jayhawk after lugging her to the doorway hatch.

"Good as I'll ever be," she remarked, staggering past him as she strapped herself into a leathery chair. "Damn was I glad to see you on the horizon. How did you know who I was?"

"Secondary reinforcements finished the raid on the rig," replied the soldier, removing his helmet to reveal a handsome chiseled face. "A contact at the DEA informed the inbound ships after the initial raid of who you were. When we reported that your body wasn't found, our source informed us it was likely that you would have gone with Nikki to eventually secure her capture. When her body didn't show up either, they deployed over a dozen Jayhawks to find out. I guess we were the ones who won the lottery. Say, was that a shark comin' for you? I've never seen anything like that!"

"It's a megalodon," Cassidy replied, turning away from the soldier and staring blankly out the window at the rolling waves beneath.

"A megalodon?" she saw the soldier ask in the reflection of the window. "Damn, I thought those sharks were supposed to be extinct. My Dad used to have a meg tooth in his office. He found it washed up on the beach. I used to be fascinated by it when I was a kid. I hope there isn't more of them? Say, what do you think about – hey, Agent Davis? Agent Davis?"

"Let her sleep, Ronny," laughed the pilot from the front. "She's been through a lot today. I'm sure she'll tell you all about it when she wakes up."

"Aye, sir," replied Ronny, closing the hatch of the helicopter with a smile.

Cassidy heard the voices around her as she melted from consciousness, dreaming about her time spent undercover, training in the firing range back at her headquarters, Nikki Salerno, the mist of the sea – and a very large set of disturbingly sharp teeth.

MURDER HIVE

1

The tumbleweed bounced off the rusted old telephone pole, rustling around the obstruction before continuing down the road. Tim Morgan sipped his coffee, watching the object bounce along down the street until it vanished past the splintered wooden border of the window.

"Needs more cream," complained his friend, David Blake, sitting across in the checkered patterned tabletop of their booth.

"Ask Peggy for more," Tim replied. "She's cool. And fast too. Not that there's a lot of people in here that would distract her."

"I don't want to bug her," David replied. "I feel like every time I come in here, I have to ask for a special request."

"It's just cream, dude," Tim laughed. "You're too nice sometimes."

The pair of old friends sat around in a diner that they had come to meet often: the Tumbleweed Diner. It was an old shack on the side of an isolated, rarely traveled highway, and a favorite stop for truckers but otherwise a business that in a few more years might be out of business.

The diner was comprised of a series of faded checker patterned booths that lined the front and back of the room, facing out through a series of glass windows that bordered both sides of the store. In the center, an old milkshake wraparound bar consumed the bulk of the restaurant – an aspect of the business that Tim thought was a waste of money. Much of the diner had an old fashioned flare; the artwork on the walls were of old photographs from around the time of the Korean War, depicting scenes of 1950's American life or photos of former important recurring customers. An old jukebox playing old Dean Martin music blared from one corner near the entrance to the kitchen, while on the opposite end near the bathrooms, an old vending machine flickered as its faulty electrical components continued to deteriorate.

But Tim and David had chosen the place to meet for convenience, not because of its charm. Tim was a college student in Tucson studying petroleum engineering. David was a member of the National Guard stationed in Las Cruces. The Tumbleweed Diner was located perfectly in between the two cities, serving as an ideal meeting place where they had lunch at least twice a year, catching up on their lives and reminiscing about their youth.

It was a Saturday morning; Tim noticed the diner looked like it often did. Counting Peggy Burke, the owner, and her husband Chet who cooked, there was a total of ten people in the small restaurant. Three people, two men and a woman, in their mid to late fifties were enjoying a hearty meal at the other end of the diner. Tim had seen them there often, thinking they used the restaurant for a similar purpose as he did for his get togethers with David.

Another woman, Michelle, was there working as a waitress. Although Tim didn't know her last name, he knew David had tried to attain her phone number once, failing miserably. She looked to be of college age, he thought, assuming her to attend school somewhere in Tucson. The pair had categorized Michelle as stunningly beautiful, albeit extremely materialistic.

Why the hell does she work all the way out here? There's no way Peggy can pay her well. Maybe she gets good tips from the truckers...

"I *swear*, if you do, I'll – you know what I'll *do!*"

"Evan, stop..."

"I *mean* it, Brandy! Try me!"

The final pair of occupants, a couple in their late twenties or early thirties, were sitting on the rear side of the diner facing the desert out back. Although the conversation was heated, the pair tried to keep their dialogue to a whisper. The loud rumble of Peggy's ancient slushy machine also helped to mask the dialogue.

"What's their issue?" David asked, trying to stir the coffee with an antique water mark stained spoon.

"They've been at it for awhile," Tim added, studying the pair nonchalantly from the corner of his eye.

The male, Evan, had on a tight fitting dark tee shirt, depicting a faded heavy metal band logo. Along his arms were fully colored tattoo sleeves depicting skulls, dragons, and other intimidating looking characters, most of which were consumed in bright fire or jagged thorns.

Brandy was equally tattooed, her hair pulled back in a tight ponytail which accentuated her rigid jawline. Even from across the restaurant, Tim could tell she was just as physically attractive as Michelle. She wore a tight fitting leathery top, and sleek pants that told Tim she could've been in a biker gang.

As Evan pointed a stern finger in Brandy's face, she slid back into her seat, almost knocking over her iced tea in fright. Veins bulged from the man's neck as he began another hushed tirade.

"I should say something," David said, his eyebrows arched defiantly. "This is ruining our reunion. He's totally menacing her! I hate dudes like that."

The footsteps of heels clicked across the diner toward their booth.

Tim looked over David's shoulder, seeing Michelle approaching with a steaming fresh pot of coffee.

"Hey you trouble-makers," she smiled behind her jet black hair. "Need another cup?"

"My friend here needs more cream," Tim smiled. "And speaking of trouble, what's up with the lovers across the diner? Ever see them before?"

"No, but I wish they'd leave," Michelle admitted, rolling her eyes. "They came in just before you two did and have been at it ever since. Thankfully Peggy took their order and I didn't have to deal with them. You know how 'no-nonsense' Peggy can be. But yeah, I'm not sure why they're arguing, but I sure don't want to get involved. That guy looks mean."

"I wouldn't mind getting involved," David replied. "That guy really needs to be taught a lesson in manners. Look at how scared that girl looks!"

Tim could tell his friend was getting angry. David's palm began to tremble and fidget as rage boiled inside of him. Tim knew it was only a matter of time before David would say something.

Peggy Burke walked over past Michelle, carrying two large cheeseburgers and fries on plates before setting them down on the table. Tim could hardly contain himself, tearing into the meal seconds after it touched the tabletop. David remained irritated, turning to Peggy.

"What's a matter', Blake?" Peggy asked, adjusting her large poofy red hair. "Don't tell me you are gonna whine about Chet's cookin' again?"

"No, Peggy, I'm sure the burger's great," David replied with a brief smile. "I'm just a little perturbed by your current clientele."

"So am I," Peggy admitted. "Awhile ago I debated on having Chet kick them out. To be honest, I haven't even given him their order yet. Depends on the next ten minutes if they calm down or not."

"I'd gladly help Chet on that," David replied.

Tim could tell from across the diner that Evan wasn't about to calm down. Frankly, Tim felt sorry for the girl in the booth. The muscular tattooed man was really giving her a nasty glare. The girl, Brandy, looked as if she wanted to be anywhere else.

As the argument continued, the three truckers on the adjacent side of the diner looked over. The tallest man, his face gaunt with age and hidden in shadow under a grimy ball cap, turned as if to confront Evan for his outrage. Pausing in mid cuss word, Evan turned and saw the trucker glaring at him, before uttering angrily, "What th' hell are you lookin' at, *old* timer?"

The trucker quickly looked back at his friends, his confidence and false bravado shattered by Evan's aggression.

"That's what I thought, asshole," Evan mumbled, turning back to Brandy.

Tim watched as a trace of rage flashed across David's face. The National Guardsman took another sip of his uncreamed coffee, before loudly setting the cup down, giving Tim a stern look.

"Sorry, Tim," David smiled, starting to stand up. "I tried, I really did."

"I got your back, brother," Tim said, standing up after him. "I just wish I could've finished my cheeseburger first."

"What are you gonna d –"

"We'll handle this," David said, stepping beside Peggy. "In the meantime, this could get a little hairy. You may want to think about having Chet grab his gun. I get the feeling that this guy might be a criminal."

"You got it," Peggy replied. "Lunch is on the house, by the way."

"A *criminal?*" Michelle said, obviously concerned. "Like how?"

"I don't know, Michelle," David replied. "I just get the feeling that he's not a good guy, okay?"

"You sure about this?" replied the nervous waitress.

"Yeah, I've seen macho assholes like this wet their pants in basic combat training. Besides, he's ruining my lunch. Peggy, do I have your permission to intervene?"

"Be my guest, sweetheart," Peggy smiled.

"Thank you."

Tim followed David around the long counter milkshake bar toward the arguing couple across the diner. At first, Evan didn't pay them any attention, until he saw that they didn't turn to the exit, but instead continued to their booth. Behind him, Peggy's shuffling was heard as she walked back to the kitchen, presumably to alert Chet that there was about to be a much-needed confrontation. Tim saw Michelle watching in suspense, and hoped that this might earn David another chance with her.

As Tim bumped into one of the bar stools as they rounded the counter, Evan turned his attention to the pair of newcomers. Captivating stares from the trio of old trucker friends looked onward, watching as a showdown was about to take place. Brandy remained rooted in her seat, looking like a deer in the headlights. A look of relief washed over her face when the pair of men arrived.

"What do you two assholes wan –"

"What the hell's your problem, man?" David interrupted Evan's remark.

"Pardon me?"

"You heard me, punk. You're being a total dick to this girl. Not to mention, you're ruining my reunion with my best friend. Cool it, will you?"

Evan stood up out of his chair, bringing his face within inches of David's. Even as he spoke in close to David, Tim could smell his horrendous breath.

"Care to run that by me again, dip-shit."

"He said cool it," Tim added, stepping to the other side of Evan, surprised by his sudden boldness. Confrontations had always been David's thing, but from time to time, Tim found himself helping out.

"What did you say, pipsqueak?"

"Cool it. Or we're tossin' your ass –"

Evan's roundhouse punch came quite unexpected to Tim Morgan as it connected with his cheek. Feeling the full force of Evan's rage, Tim felt himself flying backward through the air until his back rammed into the rim of a table.

"*Augh!*" Tim cried, feeling an ancient napkin holder and a Heinz ketchup bottle banging his back. He rolled off clumsily, avoiding striking his head on the floor as he braced himself. Luckily, he didn't have to worry about Evan's counterattack, because David Blake had moved in to engage.

Okay, let's do this!

Clenching the side of the table he had just knocked over, Tim regained his fighting stance, amazed at the brawl that was transpiring in the diner. In the seconds after Evan had thrown the first punch, David had already conducted a quick jab to the thug's ribs. Evan swung a wild spinning swipe at David's head, but David ducked, following with an extended kick to Evan's chest.

"*Oof!*" Evan cried, rolling backwards onto the floor.

Brandy had stood up with her purse and got out of the way, running over to help Tim.

"Are you okay?" Brandy asked as the fistfight continued.

"Yeah, he just sucker punched me is all," Tim replied, taking in the view.

Now that he had seen her up close, Brandy's beauty had completely captivated Tim, so much so that he forgot to rejoin the fistfight.

Ah, it's David. He can handle himself...

The first thing Tim noticed about Brandy was that she was surprisingly tall, a fact that he had not ascertained from when she had been sitting down. She stood only a few inches shorter than his own eyes, making Tim assume she was around 5'11. The corner of a rose tattoo crept up her shoulder until it vanished under her black shiny shirt – an attraction that he would normally find unattractive on a woman, but in this case, he saw it as tastefully illustrated. Her stare had him transfixed, her green eyes somewhat liberating. As she touched his shoulder, a cold chill ran up his spine. She seemed genuinely concerned for his wellbeing.

"You two really helped me out," Brandy added. "I thought he would never leave me alone."

"No problem," Tim added, shaking off his butterflies. "What's his deal anyway?"

"I'll tell you later," Brandy replied, softly removing her hand from Tim's shoulder.

"I'll freakin' *kill* you, man!" Evan roared, only to get tossed to the ground.

Tim looked back at the fight. As predicted, David's military training prevailed over Evan's street brawling fighting style. The thug was now pinned on the floor of the diner under David's thick boot. In the fight, Evan had sustained a black eye, while David looked relatively untouched, save for his slightly ruffled hair. Punctuating the fight was the heavy footsteps of Chet from the diner, carrying with him a large shotgun.

"Thank you, uh, David, right?"

"That's right," David replied, keeping his foot pressed on Evan's chest.

"Very good," Chet replied. "Mickey?"

"Yeah?" replied the other male trucker with a bright yellow ball-cap.

"Payphone outside," Chet replied, setting a quarter loudly on the counter. "Call the police, have them get up here right away. I have a feeling they'll be very interested in what we have to offer them. Might take em' awhile to get here, so I'd step on it."

"Right away, Chet," Mickey replied with a smile, taking the quarter and shuffling out of the diner.

"Get off me, asshole," Evan bellowed, pushing David's boot off his chest as he dusted himself off.

"Take a seat, son," said Chet, the sixty-year-old cook, as he prodded Evan with the shotgun barrel. "You need a lesson in manners, boy."

Evan sat back down in the booth as Tim, David, and Chet gathered around, as if guarding Brandy. Slamming his fists down on the table angrily, Evan stared out the rear window, refusing to stare back at his captors.

"You people just don't understand," Evan uttered.

Don't understand? Tim thought. *What an odd thing to say.*

"What's that supposed to mean –"

"Holy shit!" yelled one of the truckers, a female with a name-tag that read *Marsha*. "Mickey!"

Marsha's shriek of terror completely shifted the focus in the restaurant as its nine occupants turned to see what had startled the woman. The overweight woman had stood up next to the counter, pointing out through the glass windows that lined the front of the wall toward the payphone that had been installed years ago near the edge of the road.

"Marsha," Peggy asked, rounding the corner of the bar. "What are you –"

Peggy's phrase was choked back mid-sentence as the restaurant owner took in the ghastly sight that plagued the front of the diner. Everyone inside partook of the view. No one spoke, as the occupants of the Tumbleweed Diner struggled to make sense of what they were seeing.

Tim stepped away from the cluster of people to get a better look, squinting through the sunlight that poured in the windows. He could feel Brandy coming up beside him as he finally realized what was happening.

A horde of orange and black insects had descended on the area surrounding the Tumbleweed Diner by the thousands. They were everywhere – on the cars, on the large Mack truck, on the payphone, on the ground, flying in the air, and finally – viciously attacking Mickey in droves.

The trucker fought to deter the merciless insects, swatting at them with his faded trucker hat, as he cried out in agony. His defense only provoked the swarm, making several of the insects attack the man's bald head, driving the human to the pavement. As the body fell, more of the vile creatures flew in to join the attack, leaving Mickey to writhe in painful spasms on the ground. He had only ever made it halfway to the payphone, telling Tim that the police had never been called.

"What... what are they?" Brandy asked, stepping up beside him as she pressed her hand to the glass.

"Hornets," Tim gaped, marveling at the surreal scene. "Tons and tons of *murderous* hornets!"

2

"Oh my *God!*" Marsha cried, walking up to the front door with her other trucker friend. "They just... they just *attacked* him! Is he.."

"*Dead?*" asked the remaining male trucker, with a name-tag that read Nestor. "I reckon he is."

Tim could tell just from looking at Mickey's body that the trucker was obviously deceased. Even as he remained covered head to toe in clumsily crawling hornets, the trucker remained still, prostrate in the sand as the hornets continued to prod and sting the victim's remains.

Poor bastard never even made it to the payphone, Tim thought. *Which means no one knows we're out here in this swarm of hornets!*

"No one knows we're here!" he blurted out, suddenly realizing the harsh reality of the situation. "If Mickey never made the call, it means we're all *stuck* here! Stuck here with those *things!*"

"Calm down, son," Chet said, still holding the shotgun, wiping his sweaty brow. "They can't get in here. We'll just wait it out."

"There's bound to be another trucker coming down the highway soon," Nestor said, before turning back to the others. "Right?"

"Not really," Michelle admitted. "At this time of day, there's not really anyone coming down the highway by the diner. This is the busiest it's been in weeks. Typically, we're lucky if only three people are in here at this time. It could be hours before someone comes along – if they even stop by."

"That's absurd," Nestor replied, looking back at the insect infested road. "This highway runs right into Tucson. You're tellin' me that no one's gonna be comin' by here for hours? I don't believe it."

"She's telling the truth," Peggy admitted, dead-bolting the front door. "Most of the usual regulars that would stop by were deterred years ago when they put in the new Tucson business route along the highway. It runs through many shopping outlets and restaurants, which in turn, hurt our business. Michelle's right. If we're lucky, we may get one or two passersby, but it's unlikely. We might have better luck at nightfall, when the night truckers cut through here to Las Cruces. But again, that's *if* they decide to stop."

"You're tellin' me that you're not thinking anyone is gonna come in here for hours?" Nestor went on.

"It's highly probable," Chet agreed.

"There are no other phones inside?" David asked, turning to Peggy.

"Not for years," Peggy replied. "Used to have a rotary one, but the dial screwed up and we never bothered to fix it."

"Good job on that," Evan muttered.

The others ignored him.

"Are you sure he's dead?" Michelle asked, walking up to the windows. "Someone should go out there and see if he's okay. He could still be alive and be suffering."

"Why don't you go?" Evan barked. "If you're so eager to see if he's alive, why don't you go?"

"That's enough out of you!" Chet snapped. "Look, no one's going out there. If a couple hours is the worst of this, I think it's well worth the wait. This is a diner. If for some reason them bugs do stay around, we have enough food and rations for days. This is the perfect place to hold up."

"Yeah?" Tim asked, turning away from the front windows. "What if those things find a way in? No offense, Chet, but this place isn't exactly Fort Knox. Looks like it was built a hundred years ago."

"They won't get in," Peggy added. "This place is solid. She may not look like much, but she's air tight."

"I just don't understand where they all came from," Brandy said, shyly chiming in. "There has to be thousands of them too. And now that I'm really lookin' at them, they almost seem *larger* than your typical hornets."

Tim looked back out of the glass, confirming Brandy's theory. Every one of the orange bastards appeared larger than typical bumble bees, wasps or yellow jackets. One of the insects flew up to the front sidewalk of the store, allowing the humans to get a good look at it. The bug was easily over three inches long, with a lethal stinger to boot.

In the time since Mickey's demise, more of the swarm had arrived. Most of the hornets converged on the corpse, while little clusters still lingered here and there on the ground around the diner and on the road. A little squadron was buzzing around one of the Mack trucks, lured by the vehicle's chrome upper vent stacks.

"They're *everywhere!*" Marsha moaned. "They're *literally* everywhere. *Awh*, poor Mickey."

"What if they don't clear the diner in hours?" Michelle asked, fear in her tone. "What if they're still buzzing around for days? We could be stuck here for awhile."

"No one's getting stuck here," David reassured her. "Look, Peggy. Do you have any large cardboard boxes?"

"A few. Why?"

"Signs," David replied. "We can cut it out and write *HELP* on them. Then we can tape them up to the glass. That will ensure any trucker or car that *does* pass, they'll see us and hopefully bring in the calvary."

"I'd have to agree with that," Tim added. "That's our best chance at someone seeing us and at least realizing what's going on. Without some sort of distress signal like a sign, they may just pass by and think we have just a big bug problem."

"I'll go get some cardboard and some Sharpies," Peggy said, quickly rushing into the kitchen and disappearing through the swinging decorative saloon doors.

"Now all we have to do is wait," David said proudly, as if solving a complicated math equation.

"I don't think so," Brandy gasped, pointing out to the parking lot. "I think our problems are about to get a whole lot worse!"

"I don't see how that can –"

Tim choked back the words, petrified by what he saw.

As if on cue and timed perfectly with David's remark, the murder hornets that remained airborne dive bombed the vehicles in the parking lot. Tim's '84 Ford Mustang was first. The insects made a direct flight to the vehicle's tires, quickly attacking the rubber with their barbed stingers. The swarm quickly managed to puncture the first tire, quickly letting their air out, before proceeding to the next tire. When all four of the tires had been punctured, they moved over to the next vehicle – a disheveled beat-up looking minivan covered in heavy metal stickers. Tim assumed the scuffed up vehicle belonged to Evan and Brandy.

"Those assholes are blowing out all our tires!" Nestor cried, banging his fists angrily on the glass.

The diner occupants looked out the front glass, terror-stricken by what was happening. The murderous hornets descended on the rusty vehicle, quickly destroying the tires and thus rendering the vehicle a corroded piece of junk. In a rush, the mini-swarm ascended back into the arid sky, beginning another attack run on a hot-pink convertible with racing stripes – Michelle's car.

"*No!*" Michelle whined. "Why is this happening to us? *Why?!*"

"They're trying to trap us here!" Evan blurted out, with a facial expression that frowned, as if expecting rebuttal from the others.

"No, it can't be," Chet said, viewing the surreal spectacle unfolding in the parking lot.

"They are!" Michelle whined, tears running down her cheeks and diluting her mascara. "They're trapping us here!"

The hornet swarm flew off the convertible. The next target was David Blake's 1985 Jeep CJ. The hornets surrounded the vehicle in droves, with multiple smaller groups working to quickly and efficiently eradicate David's tires. A few of the hornets appeared inside the windshield, chaotically bouncing around the fragrance tree that hung in the mirror.

"I'll be dammed if I'm stranded here," Nestor barked. "If those things can get inside that car, they'll be able to find their way in this old building! Marsha, come on. We need to make a break for the truck before those hornets attack the tires!"

He made a move for the door, before Tim blocked his path.

"Out of my way, young one!" Nestor growled, putting on his sunglasses dramatically.

"Are you freakin' nuts, dude?" Tim pressed, standing his ground. "That swarm took down your friend in seconds. Those bugs are all over the parking lot and in the air. They'll sack you before you ever set foot in your truck."

"Nonsense," Nestor replied angrily. "They're all distracted by the tires and Mickey's corpse."

He paused, allowing a moment of silence for their dead trucker friend.

"Marsha and I can get away. Once we're inside, we can use the truck's radio to call for help for the rest of you. Then, no offense to anyone, but we'll be high-tailing it to the city, since there won't be any more room in the truck. If you all wait here, help will arrive. Probably in the form of the National Guard."

"I'm in the National Guard," David replied. "The nearest base is pretty far away."

"I don't know about this, Nestor," Marsha pleaded. "I think this sounds very reckless. What *if –*"

"Listen to me, Marsha," the old trucker demanded impatiently. "Those hornets will find a way inside. Before that, they'll trash all our vehicles. Our truck is still standing with all the tires inflated. It's now or never, Marsha. Do you want to live or do you want to die?"

"What's going on?" Peggy asked, coming into the large room with the cardboard and Sharpies.

"I've waited long enough," Nestor said, using the distraction to muscle past Tim. "We're heading out."

"Nestor, please," Marsha went on.

"No, this happens *now!*" Nestor said, unlocking the deadbolt. Then, before he adjusted his ball-cap one last time, Nestor flung open the door, hauling Marsha with his free arm. As the pair rushed out, Tim and Brandy quickly shut the door before any of the hornets could attack the opening. The humans rushed over to the glass, watching to see what horrors would await.

"He's not gonna make it," Evan guessed, peering through the glass.

"Will you shut up, man!" David snapped. "They're gonna make it!"

"Oh no!" Michelle shrieked, biting her long fingernails. "Here come the hornets!"

By the time Nestor and Marsha reached the halfway point between the Mack truck and the diner, hornets veered in their direction. The insect attack was fast and furious, coming from all directions as if to cut off escape from any route. Marsha was the first to feel the wrath of the hornet attack, taking a barbed stinger directly to her fleshy forearm.

"*Yaauugh!*" she yelped, flinging her elbow up wildly as she sought to swat at the insect. "Nestor, here they come! They're on me! *They're on meee!*"

"*Dammit!* I know, Marsha!" Nestor yelped as a hornet tore into his neck. "They're on me too –"

Nestor's words were cut off as ten more orange hornets latched onto his back, stabbing into him with their needle-like stingers as they drove him to the pavement. Unable to turn over, Nestor was forced to flail wildly with his face planted in the concrete, each blow missing every hornet. More of the insects nearby crawling on the parking lot leaped to the air, joining in the assault on the trucker.

As Nestor continued to scream in agony and flail uncontrollably, Marsha fared better. Using her frilled purse as a weapon, she managed to connect with three hornets that rushed her from the sky, before beginning a clumsy frantic gallop back to the diner. Two other hornets flew at her face, before taking a quick swipe from the purse.

"Unlock the door!" Michelle cried. "Marsha's comin' back!"

"Don't open that door!" Evan roared back. "You open that door and those *things* will follow her in here!"

"Evan, shut up!" David cried.

"Open the door!" Peggy yelled, scooting past Tim as she shoved back the deadbolt. She pressed open the door, letting the arid air of the desert flood into the air-conditioned diner. Marsha flew toward the opening, a swarm of the nasty hornets in hot pursuit. In the background, Nestor started a slow sluggish crawl toward the truck as another twenty or so hornets latched onto him, incessantly stabbing at his back.

He's a goner, Tim thought. *But there's still hope for Marsha!*

"Get ready to pull that door shut!" David yelled. Tim nodded, taking a spot beside the entrance, one hand on the door handle. Across the parking lot, Tim noticed more of the hornets had now broken off of Mickey's corpse, following Marsha as she bolted for the door.

"*Yeeeeaa!*" cried the old overweight trucker as she ran for the opening. In her reckless defense, Marsha managed to waylay several more hornets with her purse, but failed to deter the three that hovered directly in front of her back, stabbing into her shoulder and the back of her neck. A second later, she was at the doorway to the diner, screaming as she ran into the opening.

With a quick heave, Tim yanked the door shut, seconds before Marsha's three tormentors broke off the attack, hovering angrily at the glass blockade.

Michelle waited with a cold rag, quickly dousing Marsha's wounds as the trucker sobbed in agony.

"It was horrible!" Marsha cried, wiping her eyes. "It hurts *so* bad. Nestor, where is he? Did he make it to the truck?"

Tim looked back through the glass, past the trio of angry hornets. Nestor remained on the pavement, having crawled to within ten feet of the truck's door, and fifteen feet away from Mickey's desecrated corpse. By now, the hornets were constantly moving in between the two corpses, continuing to stab and bite, making sure the two men were deceased. Then, as if adding insult to injury, the hornets started attacking the truck's tires.

As the tires blew out, Tim grimaced, turning back to Marsha.

"No. They got him too."

3

"How do we know this is gonna work?" Michelle asked, leaning over the counter as she drew a large letter *H* with a marker on the cardboard.

"We don't," David replied, keeping an eye out the window. "But right now, it's our only shot."

Twenty minutes had passed since Marsha had returned from her failed escape attempt. The infested corpses of Nestor and Mickey were now barely visible, consumed on all sides by crawling orange and black striped hornets. In the time that passed, more of the insects had arrived, blowing out all of the remaining tires to the vehicles. Slowly, smaller clusters of the vile creatures began to encroach on the entrance to the diner, buzzing angrily around the sealed door. To make matters worse, no truckers or other vehicles had passed.

"How many signs should we make?" Peggy asked, beginning a large letter *E* on her own cardboard sheet.

"At least two *HELP* signs," David answered. "We can put them on either side of the diner; that way people driving in both directions should be able to see it, so long as the parked Mack trucks aren't blocking the view."

Peggy and Michelle continued their signs, while Chet tended to Marsha's wounds at a booth nearby, padding her neck and arms gently with an ice cold rag. David watched the door, making sure the little insects hadn't discovered a new way inside. Evan was in the corner, stewing angrily as he faced out the rear of the building that overlooked endless desert, where more murderous hornets had begun to arrive, cutting off a potential backdoor escape.

Not like it would matter much anyway, Tim thought, trying hard not to depress himself. *We'd either die from the hornets or we'd die walking in the desert sun...*

He'd previously debated on making an escape through the back entrance, but David astutely pointed out that the insects appeared to be arriving from that direction, making the matter a moot point.

He found himself on the opposite end of the milkshake bar counter, trying to trace a large letter *L* on his own cardboard strip. He felt Brandy coming up beside him, taking a seat on the bar stool.

"Looks good," she said, observing his artwork. "A little comic-book looking, but it's not like penmanship matters much with this."

"Thanks," Tim laughed.

"What do you make of all this?" Brandy asked.

"What? The hornets?"

"Yeah."

"Not sure," Tim admitted. "It's unlike anything I've ever seen. An entire swarm of hornets – odd looking ones I might add – that just randomly attack humans on sight. Not to mention, they're smart enough to trap us inside here. I'm not even sure they're from around here. They could have migrated from somewhere else. I think my biology major roommate, Chris, would have a field day examining this species."

"Do you think they'll find a way inside?" Brandy asked, shooting a timid look back at the windows.

"I hope not," Tim said. "If they do, I'm afraid it will be every man and woman for themselves."

Brandy looked over at Evan. Tim followed her stare, catching a disgruntled look from the thug before he turned quickly and stared back out the window, pretending to be watching the orange shapes that hovered past.

"So what's your story?" Tim whispered. "What's up with you two? And how'd a pretty and nice girl like yourself end up with such a dirtbag boyfriend?"

"It's a long story."

"I've got time. I've got nothing *but* time as a matter of fact."

"Okay," Brandy chuckled. "You're right about that. I guess there's not much to tell. We met in Phoenix. I was a cash-poor waitress working at a bar and grille. He was a regular, usually would stop in on weekends, but soon began to stop in more frequently just to see me. Eventually one thing led to another. At first, things were good, you know? But soon after, we started arguing, and probably drinking too much – *way* more than we should've. Things went from great, to good, to okay, to shitty pretty fast. It reached a crescendo on our way here. We had to pull over to cool off, that's when we stopped in here for some lunch. In hindsight, maybe we should've just kept on driving."

"Hey, it's not like you knew a big swarm of murder hornets would converge on the diner," Tim laughed.

"Murder hornets," Brandy smiled. "Cute name. I like it."

"What were you arguing about?"

"I'd rather not get into it," Brandy replied, avoiding the question.

"Did he try to hurt you?" Tim asked. "Or rather, has he hurt you in the past?"

"Again, I'd rather not –"

"*Hey!*" Evan bellowed, standing up from the booth. "I've had about enough of this! Brandy, I can't stand you pouring out all this bullshit about me! None of it's true. And pal, you're pissing me off even talking to her! Why don't you make like one of these hornets and *buzz* off!"

"We're just talkin'," Tim turned defiantly. "Calm down, dude."

"Don't tell me to calm down!" Evan grunted, walking briskly toward Tim.

As the thug bounded toward him, Tim stood up from the bar stool. Expecting to come to blows, Tim was surprised as Evan suddenly backed off, seconds before Chet came into view with the shotgun.

"If you're still going to be a problem," Chet said, "we can find a way to restrain you."

"Yeah," David added from the door. "This whole time you've been nothing but trouble."

"You people just don't get it, do you?" Evan scowled. "She has *all* of you fooled! Don't believe a word she says! She's not as innocent as she claims."

Not as innocent as she claims? What does he mean by that...?

"You don't seem like a sweet Georgia peach yourself," Peggy replied curtly to the tattooed man.

"Kiss my ass, old woman," Evan moaned, waving her off.

"Hey, that's enough!" David interrupted. "Now look! This is the last thing any of us need right now. If we're too busy fighting each other than working together, then those damn hornets will pick us off one by one. The best thing for us now is to finish these signs and get them taped up against the windows as soon as possible. Every second wasted here arguing is another second lost if a truck drives past. If they don't connect the dots, they'll keep driving."

"Pretty sure they'll see the two dead bodies on the parking lot and get the hint," Evan mumbled.

"David's right," Tim said. "It's pointless to argue, not when our lives are at stake from something that's out of our control. Shake on it?"

He extended a friendly handshake to Evan. The thug looked down at the hand, scowled once more, and turned back to his booth, grumbling as he went. As the tension melted away, everyone resumed their duties. As Tim turned back to his cardboard sheet, he heard Brandy whisper, more softly this time around.

"Sorry about that," Brandy said. "He can be a burden sometimes."

"What did he mean by that, Brandy?" Tim asked, eyes staying on the cardboard as he colored in the letter with the marker.

"Who knows," she replied, scooting closer to Tim – so close he could feel her thigh rubbing against his jeans which sent an icy wave up his body. "I think he's just jealous, especially when I talk to a guy I like. Don't worry about him, we're over anyway."

"You... *like* me?" Tim asked, laughing at how sophomoric the sentence sounded.

"I do," Brandy admitted, blushing. "It's not every day that a handsome guy stands up for me like you did."

"Well, David was the real muscle behind the situation."

"I'm not into army guys," Brandy laughed. "But yes, I owe him a big thanks too."

She flashed him a pleasant smile. Tim smiled awkwardly, turning back to his sign. He had considered himself an average looking guy, but was not very confident when it came to women. He had a few month-long flings in college, but nothing that stuck. Usually, meeting women was difficult for him – unlike David, who seemed to end up in another relationship every other month or so. Now that this beautiful woman was interested in him, it made him question that perhaps he wasn't so average looking after all.

Still, he thought, there was something mysterious about the dark clad tattooed woman. She was a walking dichotomy, covered in strange sinister looking tattoos, but a personality that seemed gentle and caring.

Not as innocent as she claims... He's just jealous! Still, it's a miracle she's not into David like all the other women typically are...

"So, can I have your phone number?" Tim asked, shocked by his brash confidence.

"Sure, if you give me your marker, I'll –"

"Heads up!" Chet called, aiming his double-barreled shotgun.

"Holy shit!" Michelle shrieked, biting her fake nails as she spun wildly off her bar stool.

"What?" Marsha moaned, holding the wet rag on her head as she sluggishly got up out of her booth.

"It's the hornets," Tim added, mouth ajar in crippling fear. "They're... they're dive bombing the glass."

The view of the parking lot had changed drastically. The murder hornets that previously occupied the bodies of Nestor and Mickey now took to the skies, joining several other squadrons of their airborne comrades. Then, forming in what could only be described as an aerial phalanx, the massive swarm coalesced – and then charged down at the diner's front-facing facade of windows.

"What are they trying to accomplish?" Brandy asked.

"Isn't it obvious?" David asked. "They're running suicide runs on the glass. They're sacrificing themselves to get inside."

As David elaborated on the insects' tactic, the first wave of hornets struck the glass beside his face, making him falter backwards in fright. Dying on impact, the bugs shook the glass with their pent-up momentum, before falling down to the sidewalk out of view. A second later, the second wave hit the glass, repeating the same process as their bodies fell off. The glass shook, but held.

"No way those assholes can break the window," Chet said, shaking his head. "There's just *no* way."

"Those pissant little things?" Peggy added. "No way. They're just bugs! It's glass – they can't be that strong... could they?"

A third wave rocked the glass as the hornets adjusted their strategy, choosing instead to attack one window instead of several, concentrating their strength to one area. Soon the insects selected a central area to ram – an area where a circular bullet hole from years ago remained in the window.

"What is that?" Evan muttered, rising from his booth. "Is that a friggin' bullet hole? *Jeez*, don't you people ever update this old place!?"

"*Quiet!*" David yelled, backing away from the window. "We need to move, people..."

"*Move?*" Evan whined. "Move where? The kitchen? There's nowhere to go!"

The hornets were now ramming the bullet hole one at a time, with every passing second resulting in at least four hornets perishing. Surprisingly, the hornets quickly widened the hole, with each hit chipping away more of the glass into tiny shards. Suddenly, a hornet flew through the hole, buzzing into the diner and flying straight for Marsha.

"*Ahhh!*" she cried. "Not again with you annoying bastards!"

The hornet sailed at her sweaty brow, extending its stinger toward the trucker's forehead as it bent its body – only to meet David Blake's strike from a diner lunch tray. The insect splattered on the ground, as everyone slowly backed away from the glass.

"Heads up!" Peggy yelled.

Just then, a barrage of murder hornets rushed the hole. The flying army formed a pyramid, rushing the narrow gap. The overwhelming momentum applied to the single point on the glass was enough to shake the building. Then, much to everyone's horror, the window shattered into a thousand pieces, as the horde of lethal insects exploded into the diner, sailing towards its helpless occupants.

4

How? It's not possible! It's just not possible!

Tim dove to the floor, avoiding the hailstorm of tiger-striped insects as they sailed overhead like a deadly monsoon. Several of the defenders were slow to react to the hornets breaching the restaurant. Tim attributed their lack of emotion to sheer disbelief. Under no ordinary circumstances could a normal-sized hornet swarm break glass, and slightly larger hornets shouldn't have made a difference.

But these aren't typical hornets, Tim thought as he crawled along the faded tile floor, letting the cloud of orange pass overhead. *And these certainly aren't ordinary circumstances.*

A flash of orange buzzed past his eyes as a single hornet cut off his escape, landing on the ground as it prepared its stinger. Reflexes kicking in, Tim snapped up his palm, bringing down his hand on the small creature – only to scream in pain as the stinger sliced through his hand.

"*Augh!*" Tim yelled, rolling over on his back. His hand strike had killed the insect, but not before the hornet delivered a powerful sting to the center of his palm. Blood seeped out of the wound as Tim quickly clenched the gash shut, grabbing napkins from a table to stop the flow. Sliding backward on his butt, Tim felt his spine strike the wall as he took in the madness of the room.

In seconds, the siege consumed the bulk of the restaurant as dozens and dozens of hornets flew into the dining area. The humans were interspersed around the room, trying to stave off the pests as best they could with whatever weapons they could find. Peggy grabbed a crumpled up newspaper, swinging wildly and hitting nothing. Michelle and Brandy huddled near the edge of the counter, using dinner plates to deflect the oncoming stingers. David was on top of the counter, wielding a large broom, swinging it at the hornets as they dove past on their attack runs. Chet stood bewildered with his shotgun, unable to fire off a single shot without risking hitting any of the other humans. Evan was nowhere to be seen.

Marsha!

An obvious target, Tim noticed that the large female trucker had broken off from the middle of the restaurant, heading toward the bathroom sign on the adjacent end. Many of the hornets that plagued the room chose her as the selected target. Tim assumed this to be because of her size and the wounds sustained from the prior attack outside – two factors that seemed to motivate and rally the tiny predators.

"*Augh!*" Marsha shrieked, running amok through the diner like a crazed rhinoceros.

Knocking over tables and chairs in her reckless flight, Marsha darted for the women's restroom sign, probably in hope that there were no hornets inside. A few of the nasty creatures dove at her neck, jabbing her flesh with their shiny black stingers.

"Get them off!" Marsha cried. "Get them *off!*"

"Hang on, Marsha!" Tim yelled, the closest one to the helpless trucker.

Grabbing a dusty framed picture of desert photography on the wall, Tim approached Marsha from the side, weapon at the ready. In one fluid attack, Tim brought the frame down on the bulk of her attackers, sending nearly ten hornets to the floor, crippling their wings. As he crushed them with his boot, he turned, noticing Marsha still had two hornets jabbing at her back as she made it to the bathroom.

"*Youch!*" she cried, reaching for the handle.

"Be careful, Marsha!" Peggy yelled, deflecting attacks from her own attackers. "I think the window was left open in there."

"*Auugh!*" Marsha bellowed, unable to heed Peggy's cryptic observation.

As another hornet stabbed her in the neck, Marsha yelped, involuntarily yanking open the bathroom door – only to be pummeled by a swarm of the orange pests that were waiting inside.

"*Whoa!*" David cried, swinging away a hornet. "Heads up! The room is *completely* breached!"

The sudden influx of hornets drastically tipped the favor of the battle for the insects. Stingers at the ready, the barrage of hornets stabbed Marsha repetitively in the chest, neck and face. She screamed in horror as the mob plagued the entire front of her large body, sending her collapsing to the floor with a loud *thud*. As she struck the wood, more hornets from inside the room joined in the attack. She gave out a deafening cry, dying soon after from the unbearable pain that crippled her body.

It's over! Tim thought, gripping his picture frame weapon in terror. *It's over...*

The pandemonium in the room made it every human for themselves. As more hornets flew into the room from the window, even more poured in from the bathroom. The bulk of the army flew over to Marsha's corpse, but there were still enough extra hornets in the room that confirmed what Tim feared.

More humans will die in here, he thought, swinging the picture frame at another hornet. *I'm not going down without a fight. And if I know*

David, he won't either...

"*Hiyyaa!*" yelled the national guardsman, jumping from the counter to the floor, swinging his weapon and connecting with two hornets. Beside the soldier, Tim saw that a few hornets were chasing Brandy, causing her to break away from Michelle, and toward the middle of the diner.

"They're everywhere!" Brandy cried, tears running down her cheeks, diluting her black eye shadow. "*Ow!* One stabbed my hand!"

"Watch out above you!" Tim warned, trying to battle his way to her position.

Over her head, four more hornets flew down at Brandy, attracted to her sweet perfume. As Tim arrived within ten feet of the attractive tattooed woman, several other hornets raced to cut him off. Tim paused and swung, shocked by the strategy of the hornets.

Divide and conquer, Tim thought, glimpsing the rest of the room. All of the humans now were relatively spread out, battling the insects at various areas in the room. *These little pricks are smart!*

"*Youch!*" Tim yelled, feeling the barbed point of a stinger stab his arm. Looking down, he saw one of the insects was lodged into his forearm, before awkwardly karate chopping the bug off, severing the animal at the midsection and leaving the barb stuck in his flesh. A large welt soon formed around the black splinter; a lasting reminder of what damage a single stinger jab could inflict.

Three more hornets soared at his head – only to be met with swift ends from a swing of the picture frame. The opening gave Tim another second to take in the room. By now, everyone was equally engaged in combat with their insect aggressors. Although for the most part the humans were holding their own, behind him, Tim heard a buzzing crescendo. The murder hornets that covered Marsha's corpse were now getting bored with the kill, and were preparing to take to the air and engage someone else. And as the man closest to Marsha's body, Tim knew he had to move.

His adrenaline earning him motivation and momentum, Tim arrived by Brandy's side, helping her ward off the remainder of her attackers.

"You okay?"

"Great now that you showed up," she said, flashing him a smile. "What took you so long?"

"Got held up," Tim replied, ashamed that he couldn't come up with a sexy punchline.

"Peggy, Chet, isn't there anywhere else to hide?"

"There's a management office behind the kitchen that's pretty air tight," Peggy replied. "We can try to head for there if there's not already a bunch of hornets in there. I don't know if we'll all fit, but it sure beats here."

"Let's go back – *augghhh!*"

Before Chet could finish his sentence, a swarm of hornets that had been lingering in the restaurant's rafters swooped down and dive bombed his face. He screamed in agony, passing out of view behind the counter. With a loud clang, the shotgun he had been using as a melee weapon for defense clattered across the tile floor – that's when Evan reappeared.

Leaping forward from his hiding place under a table, Evan scrambled across the room, running for the shotgun. Tim saw what he was doing and raced for the weapon himself.

"*Oof!*" Tim cried as Evan backhanded him out of the way.

"Step aside, junior," Evan laughed, grabbing the heavy weapon.

As Tim struck the ground, he looked across the floor, catching a ghastly image of Chet's deceased face poking out from around the counter. The visage was covered in sting wounds, the eyes locked in a frozen expression of terror.

"Honey, *no!*" Peggy cried, running over to her dead husband, only to be scared away by the swarm.

"Come on, Brandy!" Evan yelled, aiming the shotgun at his former girlfriend. "You're comin' with me! And don't make me ask twice!"

"Hey, get away from –"

Michelle's confidence was shattered as Evan whipped the butt of the shotgun into her face. Tim's eyes widened, seeing several teeth fly from Michelle's mouth as she was knocked backwards. She cried in agony, even as Evan roughly helped her up by her hair.

"You're comin' too!" Evan said, before pointing to Peggy. "You too, old lady. Let's go."

"Leave them alone, you asshole!" David replied. "You're not taking them anywhere. Either we're all going in that room, or we'll all die fighting out here. You're not taking any hostages. This tough guy routine – I think it's all an act."

"Oh yeah?" Evan smiled, turning the shotgun to David as he battled hornets. "Is this an act, army boy?"

The deafening blast of Chet's shotgun was so loud it momentarily scared all of the hornets in the room away from the humans – if only it came without a price. At nearly point blank range, the shotgun blast ripped through David's chest, exploding his bust in an explosion of blood. Michelle and Brandy screamed as David's blood splattered over their faces, their cries so loud it drowned out the sound of the body hitting the floor.

David was killed instantly.

"The rest of you wanna end up like this?" Evan remarked. "Now Brandy and I have a long drive ahead of us, and if things get sticky, we may need some hostages. The two of you will do perfect. Now, Peggy, show us to this private office so we can wait out this swarm."

"I'm not going anywhere with you –"

"Wanna run that by me *again?*" Evan gritted his teeth, aiming the barrel of the shotgun at Peggy's head.

"Do it, Peggy!" Michelle pleaded, blood flowing from her mouth. "He'll kill us all!"

"All right!" Peggy snapped. "Let's go. I have the key in my pocket. But please, don't hurt us!"

"Listen to every word I say and I won't have to," Evan replied, motioning to the kitchen door with the shotgun. "I'm assuming it's through the kitchen? Great. Let's go!"

5

That... that maniac! Who the hell is this guy!?

Tim crawled out from behind a booth nearest the table, seconds after he heard the saloon doors to the kitchen close. Having quickly shuffled away after Evan got ahold of the shotgun, he managed to avoid the madman's wrath. Had he been in direct eyesight of the gunman, Tim feared he may have ended up like his best friend.

Aw, dammit, Dave.

The body of David Blake was lying seven feet away, partially obscured by a few toppled tables and chairs. As Tim crawled closer, he could see that what had once been David's torso had been eviscerated by Evan's shotgun blast. Organs and bone matter spilled out onto the ancient tiled floor, coating the base of the area in a red gloss.

I'm sorry, old friend.

David's face gazed up in terror at the ceiling, as if mesmerized by the dozens of orange insects that hovered about in the rafters. Tim felt a tear leave his cheek as he beheld his friend for one last time, trying to overcome the emotions of grief and regret – but mostly cowardice.

There was nothing I could do... but I just let it happen!

Tim replayed the events through his mind, rapidly calculating different potential outcomes had he tried to attack Evan and retrieve the shotgun. But with each speculative situation, Tim didn't see an ending that didn't result with him getting shot. Evan would have been too far away to press an attack, and easily could've gunned him down too.

There was nothing... Nothing...

Tim pondered his next move. Evan had taken the three women hostage and fled somewhere behind the kitchen, presumably to the spare room. Although he had been fortunate enough not to take the brunt of another shotgun blast, his odds of survival didn't improve much. With the four others gone and Chet, David, and Marsha dead, that left him alone to evade a whole room of the irritated murder hornets.

At least the others are probably in an air tight office, Tim thought. *I have to hope that anyway. Gaugh! This is maddening... He took them hostage? Why? None of this makes any sense...*

Evan and Brandy had been fighting, sure, but the reason for the argument had never been fully realized. By the time the initial fistfight occurred, the murder hornets had arrived, ruining any chance of discovering why the tattooed pair had been arguing. As Tim crawled slowly along the floor, trying not to draw attention from the insect horde, he tried to keep his mind occupied, running through options as to what may have led Evan to act so brazenly.

Finally, he landed on one theory – the only one that made sense.

They're on the run from something. But what? Is Brandy involved? Or is she simply another hostage?

"Maybe this will give me a clue," Tim whispered aloud.

Brandy's purse sat ahead on the ground. Tim guessed that she may have dropped it when the murder hornets breached the diner.

He crawled toward the purse, keeping an eye on the infestation that lingered in the room. Thankfully, the insects had enough to keep them preoccupied. The bulk of the pests were now assaulting Chet's corpse on the other side of the counter, ramming the body repeatedly with their barbed stingers. Tim grimaced as he continued to crawl, knowing that the body of his best friend was probably next, which he wouldn't dare to watch.

The break from the attacks gave him a moment to take in their writhing forms as they shuffled along the ground or buzzed around in the air, transitioning from corpse to corpse for variance in taste. For the most part, the hornets seemed to be a few inches long, but a few of the large creatures were almost half a foot long. The stingers themselves on the larger hosts at times were two inches in length. They moved about robotically throughout the room, hovering around the human corpses, waiting their turn to feast and defile.

Orange and black bastards, Tim thought, wincing as one passed over his head before buzzing over to Chet's fleshy arm.

Finally he arrived at Brandy's purse, which had been knocked over and kicked under a table in the heat of the moment. Pushing aside a mustard bottle, Tim pulled out the object and held it into the sunlight that passed through the front windows, before ruffling through the contents.

Just what I expected. Lipstick, sunscreen, nail polish, a nail file, some wipes, hand sanitizer, some mascara... whoa!

Reaching around a crumpled up water bottle, Tim pulled out a large wad of hundred dollar bills. Every bill marked was crisp and new. A large currency strap was wrapped around the cash, indicating that fifty grand was supposedly housed in the stack.

"Holy shit," Tim murmured, looking around through the purse to find additional wads. His search turned up empty handed, leading him to turn back to the original stack. As he turned the money over, he froze, staring at what lingered on the bottom.

On the underside of the stack, a sinister red stain nearly consumed the entire bill, corrupting the pristine nature of the currency.

Blood money, Tim thought. *Evan must have stolen this from a bank or something. Figures – I finally find a girl that could be into me and she's involved with a psychopathic ex-boyfriend.*

Tim began to connect the dots, realizing the gravity of the situation that had unfolded. Evan was obviously a wanted man, possibly for murder, and definitely for something robbery-affiliated. If he had killed once before, he would certainly do it again. And the cherry on top – he now had three expendable hostages.

The only thing preventing that lunatic from getting out of here is that evil swarm of murder hornets. I can't let him get away. He could kill all three of them. I owe it to them... for David... Something has to be done. But what? The whole place is crawling with these pests.

Behind him, he could hear the hornets begin landing on David's corpse, prodding his flesh with their nasty barbs. With each stab of their stingers, an oozing sound followed, indicating blood being spilled from the wound – a sound that made Tim almost vomit.

Above, more of the hornets began crawling in the corners of the ceiling where the rafters met the walls. Several worker hornets had removed the lid of a slushie machine behind the counter, and were transporting some of the sticky residue up to the ceiling. There, the spoils of their victory was divided up – in part for food, and in part for building material that the hornets stuck to the walls. More assistants came over to help, adding to the speed in which the construction project came along. Before long, Tim was able to accurately guess what they were doing.

Damn. The little invaders are building a hive in here!

It was a thought that sent a shiver through his body. If the murder hornets intended on making the diner their new home, then it would only be a matter of time before more hornets joined in the location. Soon, the place would be crawling with the species – more so than it already had been.

And Tim was standing in the very epicenter of their new living room.

But what can I do?

His options were limited. Although at present, the murder hornets were too preoccupied with their construction and recent kills to care about him, the hornets that were still hovering around the outside of the diner were still very active. Squads of the little devils swarmed past the windows, making Tim guess that any attempt at running to the road would be met with swift retribution.

He crawled up beside the front door where the first booth had been installed and crawled below the table. Out of sight from the hornets, he was able to weigh his options.

It's either run for help, or run into the back office to confront Evan. Either way, he would have to cross huge swaths of hornets.

Neither of the options looked very attractive.

Suddenly, a loud hum began to emit on the far side of the room, followed by a sparking sound. Beside the woman's restroom, a few feet away from Marsha's bloated corpse, an old soda vending machine hummed to life, sparking against the surge strip that it had been plugged into.

Tim had seen the machine turn on and off on occasion since he had begun meeting David at the diner, making him wonder if the soda inside was any good.

The hornets must be screwing with the power lines... whoa!

The surge strip sparked again, making the front of the machine glow a brilliant white. As the fluorescent border of the vending machine lit up, the majority of the hornets in the room sprung to the air. Creating several sporadic vicious cyclones mid-air, the hornets dive charged the vending machine. So great was their onslaught that the vending machine toppled over on its side, bombarded by the combined weight of the hornet attack.

Wow, they really like light. Or hate it. Hard to tell.

Tim marveled at how the creatures quickly consumed most of the vending machine, allowing the fluorescent lighting to shine through only in sparse areas around their silhouettes.

If they like lighting that much... hmmm, I wonder...

Tim slowly stood up, deliberately trying to move slowly to avoid detection from the other insect sentries in the room. Cautiously, he shot a look outside the glass. Most of the hornets that still remained in the parking lot had moved away from the entrance, allowing him at least a small passage to travel through.

Okay, not sure when they're going to repopulate the parking lot. I may only get one chance at this, but it should be enough to fix everything – if it works!

Mentally formulating a game plan to deal with his rivals, Tim crept out the front door, beginning a short dash to the parking lot.

6

"Quiet, everyone!" Evan bellowed, waving around the shotgun as Peggy locked the door behind them. "I don't know if those hornets can hear. We don't want to lure them over here. Are you sure that thing's locked air tight?"

"It's locked," Peggy said sternly, short on patience and distraught from the death of her husband.

"Okay, good," Evan mumbled. "What about that back door?"

"It's always locked," Michelle replied.

"Good. Okay, everyone sit down."

The back office looked like one might expect from a diner that not many people would visit. It was a cramped little nook, containing a large filing cabinet, a table with a typewriter and a lamp, and a few shelves filled with stacks of dusty old muscle car magazines. The overhead ceiling tiles were plagued with water stains, and the only fluorescent light had a flickering bulb. There were no windows, hiding the occupants from what was happening outside.

"Well this is good," Evan muttered. "We can't even tell what's outside the door. These hornets could buzz away and we'd never know it. I guess every so often someone should poke a head out and look."

"Be my guest," Peggy frowned at him.

"Watch it, old lady," Evan shot her a callous look. "I'll blow your head off just like I did to that cocky asshole in the diner. I'm not above shooting you too. If I order you to open the back door, you'll do it, without as much as a *single* question. Got it?"

"Go easy on her, Evan!" Brandy snapped. "You saw what just happened to her husband out there."

"Well his bad luck is over," Evan replied. "The rest of us are still in this fight. So unless you want to end up like your husband, I suggest you play ball. Understood?"

Peggy nodded frightfully, losing the attitude while coping with her loss.

"All right, now. Everyone grab a seat, we may be here for awhile."

"What are you planning on doing with us?" Michelle said, her voice cracking as she sat down on the old tile floor.

"Depends on what happens here and how I feel," Evan replied. "If I'm in a good mood, and by some miracle these hornets leave the diner, I might take all of you into the desert. Once we're far enough away and I can sway a hitchhiker, I just might let you go. If these bugs hang around too long, they're bound to draw the attention of someone. If cops start showing up, that's when trouble starts."

"Why?" Michelle asked.

"It's not important," Evan replied.

"I think we have a right to know," Peggy added, trying to sound more concerned than stern. "If you plan on taking us hostage, we should know what you've done. Why are the police after you?"

"It doesn't matter!" came the gunman's suddenly enraged voice. "Now everyone, sit calm until I can figure this out. Okay, you! Michelle. Open that door and see if those bugs are still there."

"I'm not poking my head out there."

"Oh yes you will," Evan said, raising the shotgun.

"Leave her alone, Evan!" Brandy yelled.

"Quiet! Do it, Michelle."

Michelle stood up slowly, wiping the tears from her eyes that destroyed her makeup and foundation. Walking past their armed captor, Michelle pulled back the latch on the rear door and slowly eased open the entrance.

"*Auugh!*"

She slammed the door shut just in time – seconds before a swarm of patrolling hornets flew at the opening. As the door closed, reverberating sounds of the stingers striking the opposite side echoed throughout the room. Michelle shrieked in fright, stumbling away from the sealed doorway and nearly knocking over a stack of Chevrolet photos. Brandy deadbolted the door as Michelle wobbled past.

"*Dammit!*" Evan cried. "They've got us pinned from every angle."

As the four humans backed away from the rear entrance, a sudden buzzing from behind made them spin around. To their horror, the flimsy old hollow core door that fed from the kitchen was being bombarded from the other side.

"Oh no!" Michelle yelled, her nails digging into her palms as she clenched her fists. "They're attacking from the kitchen now!"

"If those little pecker heads can break a glass window," Evan surmised, "they can certainly plow down one of these cheap-o doors. The three of you – get up against that and hold them back!"

Peggy and Michelle obeyed without question, racing to the hollow door and bracing against it, holding the hinges intact with the old door frame as the buzzing on the other side grew louder by the second. Brandy remained rooted in her position, hands on her hips as she faced Evan.

"What about you?"

"What did you say, *bitch?*"

"Aren't you going to help? You're the muscle of the group."

"Brandy, you think I'm gonna help out and let one of you steal my shotgun? You have another thing coming!"

"I can't hold them!" Peggy cried as the loud buzzing and thumping grew louder.

"*Augh!*" Michelle whined. "Neither can I!"

Brandy raced over and helped hold the edge of the door. Splintering sounds from the other side commenced, leading the human occupants to believe that the hornets were beginning to tear through one side of the hollow core door, and would soon be able to tear through the remaining side – which served as the last line of defense.

"*Evan!*" Brandy cried. "Get over here and help! If they breach this door, it's over!"

"*Auugh!* Fine! Move aside. Let me in the middle."

Evan set the shotgun down against the office table and moved to the middle of the door. The bombardment on the adjacent side continued as the buzzing grew louder. From inside the hollow portion of the door, sounds of hornets crawling through the gap could be heard as the little insects calculated how best to turn their bodies to lay siege to the remaining side.

"They're in the door!" Peggy yelled, her hair a mess in front of her face. "They're literally *inside* the door! Oh my God, they could come through at any moment!"

"Maybe the shotgun blast will scare them!" Michelle guessed.

"That would be suicide in here – wait, Michelle! *No!*"

Brandy's pleas were ignored by Michelle who dove away from the door, springing off the entrance to gain momentum. As her hair whipped around, Evan roared in anger, trying to grab at her arm. Dodging her assailant, the disheveled waitress scrambled across the room to where the weapon remained tilted against the table. Seconds after she grabbed it, her captor pummeled into her, ruining her chances of turning the large weapon against the bulky tattooed man.

"*Help!*" Michelle cried as Evan slammed her into the wall. Somehow, she managed to hang onto the weapon with both hands, although Evan quickly did the same, beginning a wrestling match for the heavy gun. "Don't you understand? This is our chance!"

"The door won't hold if we move, Michelle!" Peggy yelled, as she pushed the door against the frame with Brandy beside her.

"*Ooof!*" Michelle cried as Evan executed a spin move, wrenching the shotgun out of her grasp while also spinning her to the ground. She landed with a loud thud, slamming into the back of the table. By the time she looked back up, Evan already had the shotgun aimed directly at her chest.

"I warned you, Michelle!" Evan yelled, pressing the trigger. "I warned y –"

The room brightened momentarily as the shotgun's muzzle flash went off, cutting off half of Evan's outburst. Michelle's head exploded in a bloody cyclone, sending fleshy red slices of brain matter around the room. The blast rocked her decapitated body backward, knocking over the remaining objects on the table, before her corpse slumped down on its side.

"*No!*" Peggy yelled, forgetting about the door and collapsing to her knees. Tears welled in her eyes as she stared at the corpse. "You killed her, you asshole! She... she was like a *daughter* to me! She didn't deserve to die!"

"Yes she did, you old hag!" Evan yelled. "What was I supposed to do? Let her get my shotgun so the three of you could take me out?"

"No one's taking you out, you idiot!" Peggy screamed. "Michelle wasn't a murderer, unlike *you!* Just because she was trying to save us, doesn't mean she would've shot you!"

"I can't hold this door by myself!" Brandy yelled over the argument. "I can feel them on the other side! They're breaking through!"

"What does it matter?" Evan said, falling back in the office chair. "Even if you hold the door, they'll tear through the hollow door eventually. At least with this shotgun, I'll be able to end my suffering."

"You miserable coward," Peggy scowled, returning to help Brandy hold back the door. "I hope it jams, and you feel every one of their stingers stab you a *thousand* times!"

"You should be nice to me," Evan laughed. "If you're lucky, I'll kill you both first before turning the gun on myself. Or maybe I'll let those hornets in here myself from the back door. They'll rush in and kill the two of you. Then I'll just sneak out when they've come through. You two will make an excellent distraction."

"You do it," Brandy said, "and you'll ruin your chances of ever finding it again."

"What?" Peggy turned. "Find *what?*"

Suddenly the ground beneath them shook with a volatile tremor, and a loud noise was heard through the walls. Evan toppled to the side, crashing into the wall and sending a messy bulletin board falling to the floor, splintering the frame. Peggy slumped against the door as Brandy braced against the doorframe.

"What the hell was that?" Evan said, regaining his stance.

"*Shhh!*" Brandy snapped. "Listen! I think those hornets are going away."

Evan paused, listening to the empty sounds on the other side of the door. Sure enough, the sounds of the hornets began to wane. Inside the hollow core door, the humans could hear the little creatures scuttling back through the holes they made, before buzzing back through the kitchen, heading toward some unknown destination.

"That was a close call," Brandy said, wiping her sweaty forehead.

"Where are they going?" Peggy asked, as if anyone truly knew the answer.

"Isn't it obvious?" Evan replied. "Whatever that noise was drew the swarm away from the door. It sounded like a pair of trucks collided on the road out there. Whatever it was, it got them off our backs. Peggy, go check on the back door. Maybe we can sneak out now."

"And what if I don't?" Peggy frowned, standing up. "You gonna shoot me like you did to poor... poor Michelle?"

"How about I show you just how much *I* –"

"I'll do it!" Brandy barked, pushing beside the two of them as she headed for the back door. Cautiously, she ran her fingernails up to the deadbolt, ramming it open, and slowly opened the door, flooding the room with afternoon sunlight.

Surprisingly, no hornets remained at the back entrance. Evan pushed past Brandy and poked the shotgun out the entrance. When nothing buzzed at the barrel, he stepped out into the sun, tactically checking his corners before turning back to the diner.

"They're gone," Evan yelled, waving them out. "Come on, let's go. If we can make it to the road, I might be able to flag down a car. After we jack it, Brandy, you know where you'll be taking me. Come on, Peggy."

"I'm not going anywhere!" Peggy said, remaining in the back room.

"Suit yourself," Evan yelled, abruptly shoving the butt end of the shotgun into her face.

Squealing in pain, the old restaurant owner collapsed on her back before rolling over. Brandy winced at the attack, knowing that if it didn't kill her, she would at least have a wicked concussion. When Peggy didn't roll back over, Evan aimed the shotgun at her static form.

"Never mind her, Evan," Brandy said, blocking his aim of the old restaurant owner. "I'll take you to it, okay? I'll take you to the money!"

"Good!" Evan roared. "If you would've just agreed earlier, we never would've had to stop at this shithole of a diner and got stuck in this mess. Their blood is on your hands, Brandy! Let's get that straight. Hey, the hell is that noise?"

From over the roof of the diner, loud squeals could be heard. The buzzing of the murder hive was barely audible over a loud cacophony of crinkling noises. Surprisingly, a column of smoke wafted over the roof, ascending to the blue desert sky. Some hornets could be seen high in the column, charging down to the source of the flames.

"Must've been one hell of a wreck?" Evan said, yanking Brandy along. "Looks like the hornets are distracted. Let's go check this out! Hopefully there's still a functional car left that we can hotwire."

Using the barrel of the shotgun to coax his hostage, Evan muscled Brandy around the building, toward the large mysterious pyre that burned on the other side.

7

"What the living hell is this?" Evan gawked, coming around the corner of the diner with Brandy.

As they came into view of the diner parking lot, they immediately identified the source of the fire. Mickey's eighteen wheeler was ablaze, sending hot shrapnel and machinery tumbling to the ground as the flames consumed the vehicle. So great was the fire that the flames leaped from Mickey's truck to Nestor and Marsha's truck. In seconds, the fuel tank of the second truck exploded, rocking the besieged vehicle back and forth on the rickety deflated tires.

"Holy *nuts!*" Evan cried, nearly tripping over a cactus.

"*Look,*" Brandy pointed. "It's attracting the swarm."

All over the parking lot, hornets dive-bombed the pair of trucks, before squealing in agony and falling to the hot concrete. More of the insects soared out from inside the diner from the broken window, flying into the flames only to perish like their naive predecessors.

"The flames," Evan smiled. "It's too attractive for them to handle. They're dying. Dying because they want to fly into the light."

Dozens of scorched hornet corpses from the earlier swarm had already perished into burnt crisps on the ground around the diner, making the parking lot look like it was covered in burned chicken wings. Soon the swarm numbers began to wane as the majority of the hive had been killed by their fatal attraction to the flames. Only a few of the flying pests now remained in the air, taking turns flying into the fire, succumbing to temptation.

"I don't understand how this could've happened," Evan said, admiring the fire that had served as the perfect distraction for the hornets. "What, did the sun just hit these tankers too hard? Golly, it is hot out here."

"The sun?" Brandy rolled her eyes. "No, dumbass. It was probably the hornets somehow. Maybe one flew into the gas tank after being covered with something flammable. They were in the diner for awhile. Maybe they got into something greasy in the kitchen and came out here."

"Well it doesn't matter," Evan smiled. "All that matters now is that most of them are dead, and we can get away. I hope the little assholes felt everything when they burned up, for all the shit they've caused."

"How do you plan on getting out of here?" Brandy asked. "Looks like they've trashed all the cars."

"All but one!" Evan smiled, looking across the parking lot.

Parked nonchalantly against an old Tumbleweed Diner sign and partially shielded by an overgrown cactus, was a rusted old Ford pickup truck. Despite the vehicle's rusty outward appearance, the sand behind the back tires revealed tread marks, indicating the truck had been driven in the last couple of days.

"It must be that old bastard Chet's vehicle!" Evan laughed, pushing Brandy forward with the butt of the shotgun. "Okay, honey, let's get in that thing n' then you better take me to the – *Oof!*"

"*Yaaa!*" Brandy cried, falling sideways from the surprise until her butt struck the side of the diner building.

Evan went down to his knees, collapsing to the ground as Tim sprang out from behind an old dumpster. In his hands he held a sturdy crowbar salvaged from inside the diner. Using the tool as an instrument of brunt force, Tim had leaped from behind the obstruction as Evan passed by. Using the explosion as a distraction – an act which he planned perfectly, Tim swung the weapon against Evan's back. Wincing as the weapon connected, Tim could hear parts of his opponent's shoulder bone shattering as his enemy collapsed to the pavement.

"*Auugh!*" Evan cried, dropping the shotgun as he rolled face up, crying in agony. "You – you broke my *shoulder,* you crazy bastard!"

Evan moaned as he rolled over for the shotgun. Tim snatched the weapon off the ground, handing Brandy the crowbar. Whining in defeat, the criminal collapsed back on the pavement among the hornet corpses.

"It's over, Evan," Tim said, pumping the shotgun. "I oughta blow your damn head off. You killed my best friend, and for what? Just because you're a trigger-happy psychopath! Now, start talkin'! What's your story, Evan?!"

"Go to hell, kid," Evan remarked, grabbing his shoulder in agony. "Why don't you ask her?"

"*Me?*" Brandy gasped. "What the hell did I do?"

"What's he talkin' about, Brandy?" Tim asked, turning the shotgun toward Evan's former lover.

"How the shit should I know?" Brandy replied, offended by the remark. "He's the one that killed two people."

"*Two?*"

"Yeah," Brandy replied. "When he took us hostage, he killed Michelle! He might have even killed Peggy when he smacked her with the shotgun."

"Okay, Evan," Tim glared down at his rival. "Start talkin'. I know you're on the run for something."

"We both are," Evan said, returning the glare and spitting blood. "For armed robbery of a bank in downtown Tucson two weeks ago. You may have heard of it. News was calling it the greatest heist in Tucson history. Things were going great – until Brandy here decided to double cross me and hide ninety percent of the money somewhere out here."

"Because I heard you on the phone, asshole," Brandy snapped. "With one of your little thugs you were working with. You were going to double cross me and take the money for yourself! I knew you couldn't be trusted. Tim, that's when he kidnapped me on this little joyride."

"If I didn't catch the money in her purse," Evan went on, "I may never have caught on – and Brandy might have been long gone with all the money, leaving me behind to deal with the fallout – she probably would've tipped off the police to our hideout after she bailed."

"Like I said, Evan," Brandy smirked. "You were going to screw me over first. I had enough. I would've split it with you fifty/fifty, if you weren't such an evil prick."

"Don't try to act like you're so innocent, Brandy," Evan smiled.

"Don't even! Tim, don't listen to him. He's trying to trick you."

"You don't want to tell Tim your little role in the bank heist?" Evan replied, slowly rising to an upright sitting position.

"What's he talkin' about, Brandy?" Tim said, turning away from Evan toward the woman.

"I have no idea, honestly!" she pleaded. "He's just making up stuff now – Tim, look out! He has a knife!"

Instinctively, Tim spammed the trigger of the shotgun. The weapon went off, recoiling back painfully into his shoulder as the loud blast ripped through the parking lot and surrounding desert region. Evan's body flew backward five feet into the soil, flailing wildly as the shotgun blast connected with his chest at point blank range, killing the robber instantly.

Tim paused, his heart beating rapidly as pain crept up his shoulder. He hadn't fired a shotgun in years, and his lack of practice was evident in the bruise that his collarbone attained.

He looked down at his victim, wincing from the sight of organs and blood that would forever stain the concrete - a reminder to the fateful encounter. Sand and pavement were visible through the hole in Evan's eviscerated torso, his face twisted in a convoluted death scream.

"Where's the knife?" Tim asked, trembling at what he had done.

"It was in his pocket," Brandy said. "He always keeps his butterfly knife there. Oh, you saved me, Tim! He was out for blood. He would've killed you, got the shotgun, and killed me – right after he tortured me into telling him where I hid his money."

"Are you sure he had a knife? Wouldn't David have frisked him after
—"

"We're wasting time!" Brandy said, grabbing his sleeve and pulling
him away. "There's still three hornets hovering around the fire that didn't
buy your distraction. There's an old truck over there. If we can get into
it, I may be able to hotwire it, then we can get out of here before the
hornets are onto us."

"Don't bother with that," Tim replied, shouldering the shotgun. "It's
Chet's truck. If the hornets left his body, I can pull the keys from his
pocket."

"*Ew*," Brandy grimaced, picturing the ghastly process. "Okay, go and
do it."

"Right. Wait here."

Tim left her, scuffling up the front of the diner. His trick had worked
perfectly. After seeing how aggressively the hornets went after the light
source of the vending machine, he put his mind to work, rigging
Mickey's eighteen wheeler to explode. The flames attracted the hornets
right to it. Allured by the glow of the flames, the horde swept into the
heat source – only to die shortly after, littering the parking lot with their
charred remains.

But the explosion also served as a distraction. It was enough to lure
Evan out from his hole in the back of the diner, and it was enough to
save Brandy from whatever horror might have befallen her after Evan
escaped the restaurant.

*It wasn't enough to save Michelle though... And Peggy? Did he kill
her too?*

Tim pulled open the door to the diner, stepping into the main
restaurant area. Just as he had anticipated, the hornets had vacated the
room completely, lured out by the blast. Hives that hung on the roof
remained half finished, abandoned in a hurry as the vile colony of
creatures buzzed away to investigate the explosion, meeting their ends
shortly after, save for the three stragglers.

"I thought this nightmare would never end," Tim muttered, walking
over to Chet's corpse.

Scarred from head to toe in swollen stinger stab wounds, Chet's body
remained where it had fallen, and, thankfully, face down. Tim
rummaged through the cadaver's pockets, wincing as his hand swept
past a few lodged stingers through the fabric. Finally, his hand clenched
on the truck's keys.

Sorry, fella. I need these more than you do right now...

A short jaunt and he was back with Brandy, who was waiting at the
front door.

"What took you so long, sexy?"

"Sorry," Tim blushed. "Felt weird reaching through a dead man's pockets."

The pair hustled across the remainder of the parking lot toward the rusted truck. Tim took note of the three remaining hornets that still hovered around the flames. They had been too scared to join their deceased comrades in the prior raid. Thankfully, they were still distracted enough by the fire that they disregarded Tim and Brandy's flight across the parking lot.

Hopscotching over the remains of the other insects and jumping over Nestor's corpse, Tim couldn't help but feel relieved, albeit depressed.

Many people whom he had come to like had been killed. His best friend of many years, David Blake, had been gunned down in cold blood. And the mysterious colony of hornets had nearly done him in, if not for his quick thinking that he attributed to his knowledge gained in the study of petroleum engineering.

But now it was all over, and he would be escaping with a beautiful woman whom actually found *him* attractive.

Maybe there will be a happy ending after all.

The pair arrived on the driver's side of the truck. Tim likened the vehicle to one of the first trucks ever manufactured. The body looked marred with time, and the underbelly appeared to be falling apart at the joints. It was a miracle the relic still worked properly.

"Here, let me hold that," Brandy said, taking the shotgun. "Open it up and let's get out of here."

"I thought you'd never ask," Tim smiled, opening the door with the keys.

Plopping down on the worn leather seats, Tim ruffled past the crumpled empty potato chip bags until he found the ignition. Turning the key, the engine roared to life after a few failed starts, which resumed Chet's old twangy country music from the speakers.

"Can't believe this hunk of scrap metal still works –"

Tim lost his train of thought as he turned to face Brandy, who aimed the barrel of the shotgun toward his face. Gone was her look of attraction and innocence, which she replaced with a scowl of determination.

"Brandy, what are you –"

"Get out of the truck, Tim," Brandy interrupted with an evil smile. "By the way, you should have listened to Evan."

8

"Brandy, are you nuts?" Tim asked, stepping slowly out from the driver's side door of the truck with his hands raised high. "What are you doing?"

"Well, you're of no use to me anymore," Brandy went on, continuing her evil grin. "Now that you've taken care of Evan for me and made sure this truck started up fine, the only thing you are to me now is a potential loose end. And loose ends are problems, Tim. Especially in my line of work."

"Your *line of work?*" Tim asked as the two changed places, with Brandy ending up near the front end of the truck.

"Yeah," she replied with a faux innocent smile. "I'm sort of a con woman."

Suddenly, moments of the day flashed in Tim's memory – Evan's warning of not to trust her in the diner, the bloody wad of cash in Brandy's purse, and recently, her declaration of Evan having a knife, despite it not having been in the robber's hand.

"Care to elaborate?" Tim said, the sting of betrayal welling in his gut.

"Sure, but only because I actually *really* do like you," Brandy joked. "For starters, everything Evan said was true. Yes, we did rob a bank and made out with quite a fortune. However, when I overheard him talking to one of his associates about stealing the money out from under me, I decided to make a move for myself. About a week ago, I pocketed all of the cash and came out here in the desert, where I hid it in a cave. My mistake was going back to our apartment instead of just bailing out then and there – you see, I left some important legal documents back in my room – documents that would've tipped off Evan to where my new house would be located after I gave him the slip. It was a big screw-up, so I went back to retrieve them. Unfortunately, that's also when he discovered the money was gone. When he confronted me about it, he saw right through me, and made me bring him out here to get it. We stopped at the diner to talk about it, since I was playing hardball with him, and that's when you met us."

"Something still doesn't add up," Tim replied, keeping his hands high. "Why were the both of you so paranoid? It was just a bank heist..."

"Oh, *ha-ha*," Brandy laughed. "That. Well, let's just say I got a little too trigger happy near the getaway car. When Evan came bolting out, he had a pair of cops hot on his tail. I had a piece on me, so I had to act quickly, otherwise they would've had us both."

Holy shit! She's a murderer! She's just as psychopathic as Evan was – if not more!

"You – you *killed* them?"

"Yep," Brandy smiled. "And that wasn't the first time. I've done this same routine a few times over the years – partner with people to rob banks only to steal the money out from under them soon after. Sometimes they get wise to it, and I've had to do away with them as well. It's become a rather lucrative scheme."

"I bet," Tim smirked, unimpressed by his captor's life of crime. "Evan didn't even have a knife, did he?"

"You catch on quick," she smiled. "Nope. Never even owned one."

"I thought as much," Tim frowned, ashamed that he reacted so brash in Evan's murder.

"I was worried too," Brandy went on. "Although Evan may not look like much, he's actually very street-smart. I fully expected him to blow my head off after he made me take him to the money. After he got my gun out from my purse, I was at his mercy. As fate would have it, the 'murder hornets' as you so comically named them, was the best thing that ever happened to me. And a bonus – they wiped out most of the witnesses that even knew I ever stopped at the diner."

"Go easy," Tim scowled. "Those animals killed a lot of good, innocent people today. But no matter how many they killed, you're still more evil than the *whole* hive."

"Watch it, Timmy," Brandy said, a hint of malevolence breaking on her smile. "I'm still debating on letting you walk out of this alive. After all, you did do me a solid in taking care of Evan for me. It's just – how will I know you won't tell anyone about me?"

"I guess you don't," Tim replied. "But I know well enough that you have no intentions of leaving me alive. You're just toying with me – just like you've done this *whole* time."

"You catch on pretty quick," Brandy scoffed. "I had you wrapped around my finger for awhile, huh? It wasn't that hard. You strike me as the type that doesn't get a lot of attention from women, am I right? *Ha-ha*, oh Tim, it's been fun playing with you, but now I think I'll – *Auugh!*"

Tim jumped back as his rival slumped forward on her knees, the shotgun falling from her hands harmlessly into the sand without discharging. Her eyes rolled back into her head as she faded from consciousness, tipping forward. As the robber known as Brandy – if that was her real name – fell face down into the dunes, Tim was relieved to see a disheveled Peggy standing behind her. An old greasy frying pan was clenched tightly in her hand.

"Order up," Peggy chuckled, delivering a horrible punchline that would've made Tim cringe had he not been so relieved to see her.

"*Peggy!*" Tim exclaimed, hugging her as he retrieved the shotgun. "I thought they killed you."

"He killed Michelle, Tim," Peggy lamented, wiping a fresh tear.

"It's okay," Tim assured her. "They can't hurt us anymore. Evan's dead. And Brandy, well, let's just say she'll have a splitting headache when she wakes up. Hopefully the cops or someone will drive past soon, and we can haul her criminal ass to jail. Apparently, she's very notorious. Not sure if you were filled in when Evan took you hostage, but turns out Brandy may have been the mastermin –"

"*Aw* hell!" Peggy shrieked. "Tim, here they come!"

Tim turned, looking in horror at the carnage across the parking lot. The three remaining murder hornets that had been buzzing around the burning trucks had diverted their attention to the human players near the truck. As if suddenly realizing that the humans had something to do with the deaths of their whole colony, the trio of insects shot over to Chet's truck, stingers at the ready.

"Tim, what *the* –"

"Get inside the truck, Peggy!" Tim cried, cutting her off.

Peggy complied with a petrified nod, diving into the truck and scooting across to the passenger seat. Tim jumped in behind her, closing the door behind him before locking both doors. Through the glass, the two watched in tantalizing suspense as the insects flew toward them. A sudden bang on the glass made Tim turn away from the insects.

"*Tim!*" Brandy shrieked, clawing desperately at the glass and pulling the handle. "Tim, let me in! They're coming! Tim, please. I'm sorry! I'm *really* sorry."

A stream of blood from Peggy's frying pan attack trickled down her cheek. Her eyes were ripe with fear as her dirty fingernails rasped at the glass. Brandy shot a terrified look at the approaching hornets, before continuing to pound on the door.

"Don't you let her in!" Peggy warned as the hornets passed over the truck. "I overheard her talkin' to you. She's no good."

"You don't have to worry about that," Tim replied, locking eyes with Brandy through the glass.

"Tim, *please!*" Brandy whined. "Please! No! No! *NoOoO!*"

The hornets reached Brandy a second later, swarming around her head with their stingers extended in jabbing positions. Stabbing from behind, the hornets punctured Brandy's neck and shoulders, prompting her to turn away from the glass and swat wildly at the vile insects. The hornets dodged her strikes with ease, using her fatigue to their advantage. With each failed swipe, the pests jabbed at her palms and hands, which made Brandy's attacks do more harm than good.

"*Auugh!* You evil little – *auugh! Auuugh!*"

Circling around their target expertly, one hornet assaulted her back, while the rest kept her busy from the front. Tim watched as Brandy's knees buckled, before she spun back around to the glass. Life waning from her eyes as she slowly dropped out of view, Tim registered her final look as a look of shock, horror – but mostly regret. Finally, her hair vanished from the window as her body sunk to the desert dunes beside the pickup truck. The hornets continued their attack, jabbing until the three pests were out of view.

"Oh my *God!*" Peggy exclaimed finally as Brandy's screams died down. "Those bugs are relentless."

"She got what she deserved," Tim replied, relaxing in his seat as he put his seat-belt on. "Come on. Let's get somewhere far away where we can warn the authorities about what happened here. I'm sure there's some wildlife organizations that would have a field day with this species."

"You don't have to convince me," Peggy replied in between sobs. "Drive, Tim. Get us out of here. I never want to see this place again..."

Putting the truck into reverse, Tim Morgan backed out of the makeshift driveway, rolling over Brandy's limp arm in the process. As they backed out onto the empty highway, Tim and Peggy shot a look back at the carnage wrought by the hive.

The restaurant was in complete disarray. Through the windows that lined the storefront, the destruction from the hornets was evident, made obvious from the toppled chairs and litter throughout. The eighteen wheeler truck continued to burn, as the flames began to crawl across the pavement, soon threatening to ignite Michelle's deflated car. The bodies of Nestor and Mickey sat adorned in corpses of scorched hornets from Tim's distraction, as did the rest of the crumbling parking lot. Lastly, Brandy's body lay sideways on the dunes. Her tormentors, the trio of murder hornets, continued to desecrate the body, adding numerous wounds to her contorted corpse.

Tim watched as the last three remaining creatures buzzed angrily around Brandy's neck. As two continued to poke and jab with the stingers, one landed on her scalp, inspecting her hair and poking at her makeup with its mandible.

"What do you suppose they are?" Peggy asked, wiping away a tear as Tim shifted into drive.

"I don't know," Tim replied, coasting away on the open highway.

"I've never seen anything like this in nature – certainly not in Arizona. One thing's for sure, there has to be more of them out there."

Driving away into the sunset toward Tucson, Tim burned rubber as Peggy came to terms with the destruction of her business and the death of her husband, crying into her sleeve. In the rear view, flames leaped from the truck to the edge of the diner, sending the ramshackle building up in smoke. Tim adjusted the mirror instead toward the open sky, refusing to look back at the burning desert crypt.

JURASSIC CARNAGE

1

"Dude, I *told* you!" came a mouthy reply from the back of the fatigued convoy of hikers. "We're freakin' lost. We've been out here for like *ten* hours! I knew I should've bought a GPS before we came out here. Shit would've only cost us twenty bucks each if we all would've chipped in."

"Buck, will you cool it?" John fired back from the front, his U.S. Navy shirt drenched in sweat. "How was I supposed to know we'd get turned around in these woods?"

"Probably because everyone in the department advised us to do it," Dane grumbled, out of breath and leaning against a rotting tree trunk. "Alten, face it, we're lost. And, not to point fingers, but Buck's right. It's your fault, asshole."

"Will you all stop bickering?" Rachel asked, swatting away a mosquito. "Gosh, these damn bugs aren't helping! I'm almost out of water. Anyone have some?"

"I have a few sips left," Vivian said, passing her canteen behind her long fake nails. "Don't hog it all. Who knows how long we'll be stranded here."

"We're not stranded, Viv," John replied. "We're just having a temporary setback. Okay, let's take a break up here and get our bearings right. Buck, let me see that map. I bet I can nail down where we're at if I can just slowly look over the topography."

If they would all give me a shot, I bet I can get us back on course in time to get out of this park by sunset.

The five graduate students halted their hike as each of them dispersed, finding places to relax among the foliage. John retrieved the map from Buck before plopping down on a withered log in plain view of the scenic valley. Although he desperately wanted to be back in the comfort of his Explorer somewhere in the parking lot, John was grateful for the brief respite. The hike had ranked among one of the most grueling tasks he had ever endured, and the whining from his peers was enough to drive anyone mad.

John Alten, the self-appointed leader of the group, was among the most well-regarded and astute students in the forestry department of the University of Montana Forestry Graduate Program. A former Navy

Reserve soldier, John joined the department after being prompted by his father that his love of outdoors could make for a promising career choice. And since his G.I. Bill was fronting the cost and thus deterring the financial burden, John thought it was a remarkable idea to jump start his civilian life.

"Another rock, Viv?" John asked, looking at her from the corner of his eye before going back to scanning the map.

"Unfortunately," Vivian replied, taking off her scuffed right hiking boot and letting the pebble fall free. "I have the worst luck with this."

"How does someone even get a rock in their hiking boot?" Buck laughed.

"When we were shimmying past that gulch," Vivian replied. "I bumped into the cleft and one must've landed right in there."

Vivian Perry, an attractive brunette who transferred to the program last fall, sat beside John Alten on the same log, patting her boot free of another small pebble. Vivian was known among the group as a prissy student, whom John assumed was most likely a former head-cheerleader in her high school days. Although she was adept at her major and usually performed well at exams, she spent most of her time whining about lack of cell-phone service than helping the group escape their precarious situation.

On the other side of the clearing, Buck Timmons, whom John likened to a former linebacker, dug into his backpack, scarfing down the remnants of a hoagie from a convenience store that they stopped at just before entering Red Peak National Park. A man in his mid-twenties, Buck was very obese. John wondered how his colleague remained so plump in a major that required frequent trips to the outdoors.

"Want the last bite?" Buck asked, his mouth dripping of Italian dressing that stained his grimy white tee-shirt.

"I'll pass," Rachel replied, holding up a resistant palm as she turned back to her fitness snack bar.

Rachel Robinson was another transfer student into the forestry program at the University of Montana. But unlike Vivian, Rachel was quiet, hiding half the time behind her dark hair or with her face buried in a text book. Although not as overly attractive like her prissy counterpart, John found Rachel's presence comforting. The two of them had talked more on this single trip than they had all semester, and John sought to get to know her better as their time together at the university went on.

"This is taking forever, Alten!" whined Dane. "If you can't figure this shit out I'm gonna go *bat-shit* insane! I can't believe we trusted you to lead us on this trek. We've been lost out here since morning."

"Cool it with the melodramatics, Dane," John scolded, leering at his companion. "We've only been out here eight hours. It's not my fault if you already drained your canteen. Besides, I can hear a creek up ahead. Replenish there if you're still thirsty."

"It's not that I'm thirsty, dick-head," Dane grumbled, tying his boot strings tighter. "It's that I'm annoyed at why we let you call all the shots. We would've found him by now if we had let me lead the way. You're gonna get us all a big fat F on the assignment."

"I'm gonna pretend you didn't just say that," John replied, turning back to the map.

Dane Wells was the proverbial smart ass of the group. Throughout their undergrad years in the forestry program, John Alten tried his best to steer clear of Dane Wells. Dane was someone that John classified as an alcoholic, a brawler, and a buffoon. John also thought it was nothing short of a miracle that Dane had lasted this long in the program, wondering if his class rival would've intimidated the professors into letting him pass.

They should've never even given him his bachelor's degree, John thought, studying the map.

Unfortunately, as fate would have it, Professor Richard Slovak put the two together in yet another hopeless class project. Now, along with three other students, the pair would have to find a way to get along – or at least try not to kill each other until they made it back to civilization.

"*Ugh,* these freakin' bugs are *everywhere* up here!" Vivian lamented, swatting another nosy mosquito. "Worst of all: there's no cell service! That's more than infuriating!"

"*Viv,*" Buck began sarcastically, wiping his fleshy jaw free of Italian dressing. "How do you plan on a career in forestry if you can't even stand the bugs?"

"Well because I like the cute little bear cubs and foxes," Vivian smiled, checking her bright red lipstick in her glitter-encrusted compact mirror. "But get real, I don't think anyone really cares for the bugs, am I right?"

"I know I could do without them," Rachel nodded, crumpling up her energy bar wrapper and stuffing it into her backpack. "I still can't believe we're lost out here."

"For all we know, so is Professor Slovak," John replied. "We tried shouting a dozen times. That guy knows the outdoors like the back of his hand. He would've shouted back if he was anywhere in earshot. He could be even more lost than we are. If we make it back and his car is still at the parking lot, I'm putting in a missing persons report."

"That's stupid," came Dane's curt reply. "He's out here somewhere. Something tells me we'll be running into his goofy ass soon enough."

Professor Richard Slovak had chosen the five students at random to go on an excursion through Red Peak for several reasons. For one, the expedition served to illustrate to the students just how rugged the Montana terrain was, which would be helpful if the students chose to pursue a forestry career in the same state. Another reason, Professor Slovak believed that other forestry classes were too classroom-oriented, and he occasionally enjoyed assigning projects that involved field experience. Finally, Professor Slovak tried to instill in them the pride of working as a team – a goal that had yet to be attained.

Other students in the class had been assigned to simple wooded regions all throughout the state during various weekends. John Alten's group drew the short stick of the deal when Professor Slovak assigned them to Red Peak, a national park known for its endless web of mountains and pine forests – and frequent missing people that never returned from hikes.

John shrugged off his doubts of being lost, folding up the map and handing it back to Buck.

"Any luck?" Buck asked, his gut sagging down from his tight polo.

"What do you think?" John asked, sipping his canteen as he flicked the map. "The map is a Jackson Pollock masterpiece of shades of green. I don't even know which mountain we're on. They all mesh together too well. It's not surprising that so many people go missing up here."

"Well that's not gonna be us, right John?" Vivian asked, her lips pursed in a worried smirk.

"Course not, Viv," John laughed. "What kind of forestry students would we be if we can't get out of this? Hell, this is probably Professor Slovak's hidden lesson: find your way out of Red Peak without driving yourself stark-raving mad."

I sure hope we get out of here before sundown...

"Please," Rachel laughed, rising up and stretching. "Nothing against Professor Slovak. He has great class lectures, but he's not the "find the hidden meaning" type of teacher. He's very practical and always explains his lessons up front. I'm think you're right though, John. Maybe he is lost too."

"That's what I'm afraid of," John replied. "And who could blame him? I'd bet even the ancient Native American tribes would have problems in these foothills. Jeez, I feel like we've been walking in circles for hours."

"That's because we didn't bring a GPS, dumbass," Dane remarked, spitting out his snuff on a fern.

"I've had about enough of you, Dane," John replied, taking a step closer to his opponent. Dane returned the maneuver, positioning his unkempt stubble within inches of John's face.

"Careful, Alten," Dane replied with a challenging grin. "Out here, it's just you and me."

"A breath-mint might do you a favor, scumbag," John smirked, eye to eye with his antagonist.

"Hey, *shhh!*" Vivian exclaimed, standing up. "Did y'all hear that?"

Vivian's sudden alertness gave pause to the climactic argument. The group listened, although all John could hear was the tranquil mountain breeze rustling under pine needles. In the valley ahead, the cry of an eagle carried over the slope, but no other discernible noises were heard.

"What, Viv?" John asked, irritable from the long overdue standoff with Dane. "What did you hear?"

"I don't know," she answered honestly. "It sounded like some moaning. *Wait!* There it is again! Come over here. I think it's coming from down the path here."

The four graduate students huddled around Vivian from her place on the log. Sure enough, down the trail came a distant guttural gagging sound. Labored coughing followed. Whoever the caller was, it was apparent they were in peril and possibly injured. Soon, the whine became a cry, as the caller wound up the energy or courage to cry an exasperated, "*Help!*"

"Sounds like Professor Slovak!" John announced, hastily snatching up his backpack. "He's in trouble!"

Boots pounding the trail, John bolted down the path. Behind him, he heard the four others scramble for their items before following the former veteran further into the brush. Adrenaline pumping through his veins, John worried that his instructor might be too injured to walk back. Carrying the man would be a burden, but would have to be done, since the cell service was still out. Of course, even if they could move him, they would have to discover the way back to the parking lot.

Maybe we'll be lucky and run into some forest rangers who can help...

Suddenly it was all making sense. Professor Slovak never linked up with the students because he had been injured, probably on behalf of a nasty fall down one of the many serpentine paths.

Or maybe sprained an ankle on a rock; struck his head and passed out.

In the complex web of woodlands and trails that comprised Red Peak, the possibilities were endless as to why Professor Slovak might be in trouble. But when John finally arrived at the scene, his theories suddenly took a turn for the surreal.

"*Holy cow!*" John exclaimed, winding around the corner of a rocky buildup.

Professor Slovak was lying in the center of the trail, his body torn to shreds at the abdomen. Guts and intestines emptied out onto the earth, staining the dirt and nearby boulders in their crimson sinister coating. His face was pale, twisted with a look of panic and delirium. A faint glimmer of a smile crossed his face as John ran up to him, cradling his head.

"*Alten,*" came the croaky reply as Professor Slovak stared at his student behind his wide-rimmed glasses. "Good to see you, soldier."

"Professor Slovak, what happened?" John asked, trying to overcome shock as his four companions trudged up behind him. "Was it a bear? A mountain lion?"

"*Jeez,* oh man!" Buck cried, barfing the remainder of his hoagie off trail. "What the hell, John!"

Behind him, John could feel a shift in emotion creep over his classmates. Vivian started to weep as Dane blurted out offensive profanities. Rachel was silent, gripping a nearby tree in fright. The eyes of their dying instructor locked with John's, welling with the tears that undoubtedly came with traveling to the mysterious next life.

"*Alten,*" Professor Slovak went on, blood seeping out from his pale, quivering lip. "No. It wasn't a bear. It's... it's still up here, *Alten.* You have to get your friends out of here... It will come... *back!*"

"*It's? What does he mean?*"

"What's up here?" Dane asked. "What was it, Professor?"

"*Run,* kids!" the professor gasped, his mouth agape with fright. "*Just... run...*"

With that, Professor Slovak died, his head going limp in John's hand. An ominous silence fell over the group as John rested the cadaver's head back down on the rock. Dane was the first to speak.

"Well that was cryptic as hell!" he blurted out, seemingly unphased by his instructor's demise. "What did he mean by that?"

"Maybe you can show some sympathy, Dane!" Vivian snapped, wiping flowing tears. "Our *freakin'* professor who we've come to know and love just died! Who the hell cares what he meant –"

"Oh, hell no!" Buck swore, stumbling backwards on a log.

At that moment, a massive roar rippled through the mountains, cutting off Vivian's sentence midway and making the five students freeze in terror. Birds leaped from the perches high above, taking to the sky in a massive flock to avoid coming into contact with whatever made the mighty growl. It was a sound unlike anything John had ever heard – he likened the sound as a mix between a lion and a powerful locomotive. Whatever it was – it was undoubtedly the unchallenged apex predator of the region.

And it was close by.

2

"What the hell was that?" Vivian asked, huddling behind John as the primordial growl reverberated throughout the valley.

"How do you expect us to know, Viv?" Buck asked, looking about wildly for the origin of the growl. "*Jeez*, oh man, that sounded close! John, you're a former veteran. Any idea of where it came from? How close it was?"

"I was a soldier, Buck," John replied, searching the trees for signs of movement. "Not a psychic. It's close though. Gun to my head, I'd say under a mile."

"No shit," Dane spat, masking his fear with false bravery, "How close? There's five of us. Come on, Alten. We can take this thing!"

"No," John replied bluntly, keeping his stern gaze fixed on the trees. "No, we can't."

"Alten, what are *you* –"

"Look at the body, Dane," John answered, gesturing to Professor Slovak's devastated remains. "Take a look at the midsection. There's at least two teeth lodged in the torso. Get a load of them. Several inches long. Serrated. Yeah, whatever this thing is – none of us will be able to take it on. It'll rip us to shreds."

"Alten, you're yankin' my chain," Dane grumbled, brushing past John as he inspected the professor's gruesome cadaver. "No way in hell there's any tooth that *bi* –"

Dane paused, entranced by something lodged into the victim's chest. Then, reaching forward cautiously as if expecting to get sliced by the foreign object, he plucked up what resembled a large sharp white rock. The object was about the size of his palm. Dane dropped the object, haunted by the realization that whatever killed Professor Slovak could dispatch them with ease.

John snatched up the tooth, inspecting it before putting it in his pocket.

"What do you think it was?" Rachel asked. "A bear?"

"Could be," John replied. "But if it is, it's the biggest bear I've ever seen. I'm talkin' bigger than an extinct cave bear. Might as well be a Sasquatch tooth for all I know."

"A *Sasquatch?*" Dane said, rolling his eyes.

"Yeah, Dane!" Rachel snapped, suddenly gaining confidence. "Why is that so hard to believe? You've heard of all the people that have vanished in Red Peak over the years, and no one could ever find any trace of them. What makes you think it's such a ridiculous notion to think there may be large animal predation at work?"

"I *don't* think it's a ridiculous idea," Dane replied with a scowl of contempt. "I just think it's foolish to think a 'squatch could've killed Professor Slovak."

"Why?" Rachel went on. "We've only been in North America for how long? Four hundred, five hundred years. Is it so crazy to think something like a Bigfoot might be out here that we haven't discovered yet?"

"It's not a 'squatch," John interrupted. "It's something bipedal sure, but it's most likely reptilian."

"How can you be sure?" Buck asked. "And what's bipedal mean?"

"It means whatever it is, it walks on two legs," John replied. "And how do I know it's a reptilian? Simple, that's how."

John Alten pointed down the trail. Hidden in Professor Slovak's cascading waterfall of blood, a single footprint remained imprinted in the moist earth. As the students huddled around the ominous impression, it was undeniable that the creature was reptilian by the sharp triangular claw patterns at the front. The impact caused by the animal impressed the track several inches into the ground, indicating an animal of immense weight. Buck staggered backward in fright, shocked by the scale and depth of the track.

"Dude," he said, fiddling with his university ball cap. "What kind of animal on Earth makes tracks like *that?*"

"Not sure," John replied. "Unless, like Rachel pointed out, there's large lizards around here that none of us know about, because it's rare that people actually come up this far into the park."

"Guys," Vivian moaned. "I'm like freakin' out here! Why can't we like, just go?"

"Go where?" Dane asked. "We're lost! If we start running off in some random direction, we could run right into the scaly bastard and never even know it until it's too late!"

"*Whoa!*" Buck screeched, almost wobbling over.

A loud footstep crashed through the trees, this time unmistakably to the right, where the trail continued to feed from where Professor Slovak was traveling before he died. In the distance over a hundred yards away, a tree crashed over through the thicket, slamming into the earth with powerful force. Whatever knocked over the tree took another step toward the students' direction, following up with an impressive, mighty roar that mirrored the first growl moments earlier.

"Oh no..." Vivian moaned, collapsing to her knees. "Oh no, *no no...*"

"Come on, Viv!" John cried, reaching under her armpits and yanking her off the ground. "We can't stay here! That thing's gonna be comin' through here again!"

"Where do we go!" Rachel asked, already turning to run.

"*Anywhere!*" John yelled. "Anywhere but here. Go, *Go!*"

He shoved Rachel away into the forest after the three others, leaving the body of Professor Slovak to decay over time in the desolate mountain path.

#

"What the hell, John!" Vivian screeched, eating a face-full of pine needles as she pushed through the branch. "What is it?"

"I don't know, Viv!" John cried, brushing shoulders with a splintered trunk. "I didn't see it. Just keep running! I don't know if it's still following us."

"It's big enough to knock down trees!" Buck cried, tripping over a twig and face-planting in the dirt.

"Is it still behind us?" Rachel cried, eyes filled with fright.

John cast a look back. To his horror, he saw another tree topple over through the foliage, crashing into the ground and sending the impact tremor rippling under their feet. Rachel heard the sound, spinning around as if to get a view of whatever was chasing them, before turning back to the path ahead.

What is it? What in the hell is it?

John racked his head trying to form an image of what type of lizard may be chasing them, but the largest he could come up with was a Komodo dragon. And Komodos weren't from America, and they certainly couldn't walk on two feet, at least not for long, nor could they dislocate trees with minimal effort.

But what kind of lizard can? Basilisks? Frilled lizards? They're nowhere near the size of Professor Slovak's killer.

In their fearful sprint through the thicket, John noticed that they had gotten off course again, traversing through a different route that they had previously arrived through. Not that it mattered much to John – they were lost already, and any direction away from the monster was good enough for him.

Monsters, he thought, trying to make sense of his disturbing reality. *Monsters in Red Peak?*

As implausible as the thought was, it certainly *was* a monster that murdered Professor Slovak. Based on the size of the tooth that he still felt stabbing him through the pocket, John guessed the phantom monster was at least twelve feet tall, much taller than a bear or mountain lion. And a bear that could knock down trees?

Unlikely, John thought, pushing through another pine branch barrier.

"*Stop!*" Buck whined from John's left, leaning against a tree. "I *have* to stop! I can barely... catch my breath..."

"Come on, fat ass!" Dane scolded him, although fighting for breath himself. "That... big-ass monster will be on us in minutes if we don't move!"

"No, I have to stop too," Vivian managed between her dramatic breaths, pressing her fake nails into the bark of an old tree as she struggled to remain upright. "Dane, stop, will you? I'm *literally* gonna pass out!"

"Push yourself, princess!" Dane bellowed. "Do you all wanna live or *die?*"

"Shut up, Dane!" Rachel snapped, growing tired of her classmate's deplorable behavior. "Shit, it's still comin' this way!"

With an earth-shattering crack, another tree trunk two hundred yards to their rear splintered in the middle. The upper portion of the trunk fell to the earth, crashing through several other neighboring tree branches in the process. Barely visible through the ranks of pine trees, something stirred under the shade of the conifers, barely visible among the camouflaging wooded environment.

"I saw it!" John gasped, pointing to the jungle of identical conifers.

"Me too!" Rachel exclaimed. "It's *big!*"

"What is it?" Dane asked. "Dammit, will someone tell me what the hell this thing is!"

"I don't know what it is, Dane!" John shot back. "It's just big and dammed hard to see! It's hard to tell from this distance, but I think it's green in color. Makes it easy for it to blend in with its surroundings. For some reason, I think it's toying with us."

"What?" Buck whined. "So what is it; a big iguana?"

"I don't know," John answered. "Get behind that log, dude, or we're done for!"

Clenching the bark of a rotting tree log, John Alten felt fear and adrenaline flowing through him at a rate that he had not felt since his basic combat training tenure in the Navy. His palms riddled with splinters from the ancient pine wood, the veteran kept his gaze transfixed on what lay ahead as more trees continued to shake and fall, signaling the imminent approach of their dreaded pursuer.

Around him, the four other graduate students gathered, two on either side, watching in tantalizing suspense as the trees ahead continued to sway. John gritted his teeth in anticipation, knowing that his combat training gave him the endurance to keep running if the worst happened.

The others... I can't leave them. Especially Vivian and Buck. They're too out of shape for this...

"Keep your head down," John warned the others, seeing that all obeyed – except for Dane Wells, of course.

"Where is it, Alten? I can't see it!"

"*Dammit*, Dane! Seeing it isn't important right now. What is important is keeping out of sight."

"What if it corners us here?" Vivian asked, tears flowing down her cheeks and laying waste to her blush makeup. "What if it does to us what it did to Professor Slovak? What if it gets *me* last?"

"It's not gonna get us, Viv," John replied, ignoring his colleague's selfish but well-meaning statement. "Just think positive and stay low. It'll pass by, then when the coast is clear, we'll continue into the woods in the opposite direction that it left in. We're gonna make it through this!"

"Except we have no idea where the hell we're *actually* going, Alten," Dane added. "What's the use of avoiding this thing if all we're going to be doing is heading further into the state park? We need to find out where there's a ranger station and head for it."

"No shit," John replied. "Except we don't know where one of those stations are at. One thing at a time, Dane."

Another tree a hundred yards away cracked as something massive brushed alongside its base, sending pine cones and needles showering down to the earth. A fierce guttural roar rang out through the grove, as a pair of hidden squirrels scurried up a tree trunk, vanishing into a hole notched in the bark. The footsteps of the mysterious beast grew loud, each step adding more intense ground tremors that rippled under the students' hiding place.

"*Jeez*, it's big!" Buck whispered, holding his chest as if to calm his runaway heart rate. "I think I'm gonna have a panic attack, Alten! This is too much, man."

"Keep it together, Buck," John snapped impatiently, refusing to look away from the trail ahead.

"Holy shit, Alten!" Dane remarked, peeking over the log. "I can see it!"

"What?" Rachel whispered. "What is it?"

"Get down!" John replied, as Vivian and Rachel prepared to look over.

"Oh my God!" Dane went on. "It's...It's as *big* as a *freakin'* mobile home! I can see glimpses through the trees... Alten, you need to see this..."

"*Ugh!*" John winced, appalled by the lack of street-smarts employed by his colleagues.

By now, everyone except for John was peering over the top of the log, gawking at whatever was approaching through the thicket. John saw Vivian's expression shift from terror to awe, her jaw agape at whatever lurked toward their crude hiding place. Dane looked like he had seen a ghost, and Buck was so nervous that he became loudly flatulent.

"If it couldn't smell us before, it certainly will now," Dane frowned, covering his nostrils. "Nice one, Buck."

"Keep your heads down, dammit –"

John cut off his own order as he lifted his head slightly, inadvertently achieving a view of the pine forest that loomed to their forefront. In the process, he unknowingly inherited the same mesmerizing vision that the others received, and in turn, became equally entranced.

It was a vision that he had not seen since he was a child, when his parents bought him VHS tapes of his favorite prehistoric documentaries. The content within those old films gave him a firm understanding of ancient animal life, imprinting in his mind scientific terminology that he would never forget.

"What is it?" Dane asked.

The green shape drew closer under the trees, bobbing into more pine needles that rained down on the animal's bulky shaded silhouette. As the reptilian figure passed under a sunny portion of the trees, the group was able to get a definitive look at the beast, giving John the sighting he needed to confirm his absurd, yet accurate theory.

"It's an allosaurus!" John gasped, clenching the log so tightly that his fingernails bled.

3

"An *Allo – what?*" Dane asked, raising a skeptical eyebrow.

"It's an allosaurus," John repeated himself. "An apex predator of the ancient Jurassic period. Obviously they were thought to be extinct, just like all the other dinosaurs. Apparently, some must've survived here in Montana. They're savage killers."

"Are you saying it's a *freakin'* T-Rex?" Buck whimpered, a wet spot forming on his blue denim jeans.

"An allosaurus," John repeated for a third time. "Yes."

"A... a *dinosaur?*" Vivian asked.

"Yes, Viv. It's an actual dinosaur."

As if approaching their position like a slow-moving drug sniffer dog, the allosaurus pushed through the last patch of shade, arriving in a glorious spot where the sunlight shined through, illuminating its alluring skin coloration. Standing over fifteen feet tall, the Jurassic carnivore was comprised of green and yellow scales, making it the perfect hunter in the pine forests of the Red Peak National Park. Stark contrasting dark green blotches ran down the back of the creature, starting from the skull all the way to the tip of the tail, reminding John of an abstract version of a Bengal tiger pattern. Rows of glistening white teeth, although stained by Professor Slovak's blood, glistened under the sunlight. Lastly, the golden eyes of the creature glowed like two precious gemstones, captivating the students with their wicked, sinister luster.

"We gotta get out of here," Buck stammered, ducking back down. "We... *I*... I *gotta* get out of here!"

"Stay down!" John ordered. "It hasn't seen us yet!"

"The hell it hasn't," Buck spat. "It's comin' straight toward us, Alten!"

"Buck, don't be a fool!" Rachel added. "Be real. Do you really think we can outrun that thing? Its legs are *bigger* than you! We're exhausted too! That thing's basically been walkin' after us and it's kept up! If it starts running, it's over, Buck."

"Rach, I can't take this, I *can't* take this!"

"Shut up, *fat boy!*" Dane hissed. "Your blubbering is gonna lead it right to us. It's almost here!"

Sniffing at the mountain breeze with its massive flaring nostrils, the allosaurus pressed its green snout to the earth, easily scooting aside rocks with its bulbous head. Mists shot out from the dinosaur's angry nose like a medieval dragon as the creature sought to determine where its targets had fled to. With a wag of its long tail, the carnivore knocked off several low hanging branches of a conifer to its rear. The allosaurus turned to inspect the sudden noise, before turning back to sniffing the trail. John estimated the dinosaur was less than thirty yards away.

"Dude, it can *smell* us!" Dane whispered as the five students crouched back under the log. "You didn't tell me it could hunt by smell, Alten! I thought these things hunted by sight."

"They were thought to be extinct for millions of years, Dane!" John hissed. "How the hell am I supposed to know how they stalk their prey?"

"It's stalking us?" Vivian asked. "Oh, God! What are we –"

"I knew I should've brought my gun," Dane interrupted, pounding his fist on the mossy earth. "At least then we'd have a fighting chance."

"So what do we do now?" Rachel asked. "That dinosaur's gotta be over fifteen feet tall. It can probably see us a quarter mile off."

"It could," John agreed, "if we didn't have all the trees and bushes for cover. Now that we know it hunts by smell, it's imperative that we move! Dane, you're the closest to the left. That way bleeds downhill to the flat lands. Start crawling."

"Why do I have to – "

"*Dammit*, Dane!" Vivian snapped. "Move your ass. The dinosaur is just over the log."

"*Jeez*, fine! But don't order me around again!"

Dane began a hurried crawl across the shredded leaves and pine needles, using his hands and knees to shuffle away from their log of cover. He cast a look backwards, confirming that the dinosaur was still busy rooting around in the clearing, before he vanished from view, descending down the slope. Vivian followed quickly. John and Rachel were right behind her, with Buck bringing up the rear.

As he winced as pine needles and loose rocky topsoil plagued his hands with cuts and bruises, John struggled to hear what was happening back up on the ridge. The allosaurus was quiet, presumably still sniffing around the clearing for the missing five graduate students.

Is it toying with us? Surely it has to know we're close by.

A top predator in the Jurassic period, John tried to second-guess his theory. An allosaurus, alive and well in Montana.

It has to be something else...

Yet nothing else made sense. The creature was as large as an allosaurus, and was unmistakably a massive carnivorous theropod.

Has it survived all this time without anyone knowing simply by hiding in the park? Or is it a cloning experiment gone wrong? God knows our government probably has the power to bring these creatures back...

After a minute of quick crawling and zig-zagging down the hill, Dane arrived at the base, rolling behind a pine before standing and shooting a look back up the hill.

"Do you still see it?" Vivian asked, arriving at the flatland and standing up herself.

"No," Dane said, peering up the hill. "Can't see anything up there. Maybe it went off in the other direction. Maybe good ol' Buck's fart mixed with the wind and confused it."

"Dude, I don't want to hear it," Buck whined, trying to hide his urine stain on his pants as he arrived with John and Rachel at the base. "It's not every day that I'm hunted through a national park by a big dinosaur. And that Italian hoagie messed me up."

"Do you see it?" Rachel asked John as he turned, glimpsing the hundred feet back up to the hilltop.

"Nope," John replied. "Dane's right. I think it's still dickin' around up near the log."

"Where do we go from here?" Rachel asked. "Straight ahead?"

"Down to the lowlands," John replied. "Increases our chances of running into a forest ranger access road. If we're lucky, we'll run into one of their Jeeps. Then they can take us back to the station, or ideally out of the park altogether."

"I'm all for that," Buck said. "Or anywhere but here. Lead the way, Alten."

They began a brisk jog away from the slope. Constantly double checking over their backs, the graduate students still saw no sign of the elusive dinosaur at the summit. Several minutes later, the top of the hill was out of view, replaced with a dense thicket. No further sounds of the allosaurus' massive footsteps came from the forest, and the roars of the carnivore had ceased.

"This has gotta be the find of the century," Dane announced, whispering at first as he looked over his shoulder again. "When the five of us get back to civilization and report what we've found, we'll be famous! We'll be on every news outlet. I'm talkin' movies and documentaries! National Geographic; that kind of thing."

"Let's worry about getting out of Red Peak first," Vivian said, examining her broken nails as she almost ran into a tree.

"I'm serious, Viv," Dane went on, again cautiously looking back at the trail. "This could change our lives! Screw finishing our degrees! The five of us have a whole life of interviews and public speaking engagements lined up."

"Or no one will believe us," John replied bluntly.

"What do you mean, Alten?"

"What I mean is that no one will believe us if we don't capture the dammed thing," John went on. "Think of it. Did any of us think to snap a picture of the dinosaur? Nope. All we have to show for it is this one tooth I pulled off from Professor Slovak's body."

"If there's enough people combing these hills, I think it can be captured."

"I wouldn't be so sure on that, Dane," Rachel added.

"Bullshit."

"No, really. This thing has been here for how long? Millions of years. Montana's been a state since 1889. So over a hundred years with all these people, and that whole time this dinosaur has been hidden."

"Oh, I'm sure it's been having run-ins with people for awhile now," John replied. "The problem is, of course, that no one ever lives to tell about it. And with the increased urbanization and deforestation of the state, I have a feeling these run-ins will become more frequent. And where there's one of these things, there must be more of them."

"*More* of those things?" Vivian winced, shivering "*Ugh*, so slimy! *Ugh!* I can't wait to get out of this place. John, any idea of where to go?"

"Not really," John said, checking his compass. "Right now we're headed due east. I don't know where the last ranger station was, but we may end up leaving park grounds before then if we keep headin' in this direction. We arrived at the east end of the park. It's probable we'll even hit a main road soon if we don't stop."

"Yeah, except this park is so oddly shaped," Rachel added. "We could be walking east for a very long time. Shitty thing is – it'll be dark in a few hours."

"*What?*" Vivian said, pausing. "Oh my God! I've completely lost track of time. We need to get out of this park *now!* I cannot be bumbling around here in the dark with this *thing* on the loose!"

"Well I think I speak for everyone when I say this," John began, "but I have no intention of going to sleep at night. We have a pair of flashlights with us. I say we keep going as long as we're able. I don't think any of us are gonna get a good night's sleep here, now that we know what's at stake."

"Agreed on that, Alten," Rachel replied, swatting away a branch.

Alten, John thought. *That's the first time she's really called me the class nickname.*

Out of the four other people in this life or death predicament, Rachel was the bravest. Unlike Vivian who was too frazzled, Buck who couldn't stop going to the bathroom, or Dane who was mouthing off any chance he got, Rachel was very cool under pressure. It was a trait he had come to appreciate from his peers in the Navy. If they made it out of this alive, John vowed to make more of an effort to befriend her, if not even ask her out.

I don't think she's with anyone, is she? Ugh, damn. Should've made more of an effort to talk to her between classes. I spent all that time being interested in Vivian. What a waste of effort that was.

"*Wait!*" Vivian said, stopping short at the front of the group. "Something's not right."

Her ominous remarks made them halt, shifting the positive tone of the group. Breathing laboriously as he tried to ward off a panic attack, Buck looked around in terror. Dane stepped up in front of Vivian, bearing a look of annoyance.

"What did you mean by that?" he asked with a scowl.

"I don't know," Vivian replied. "I'm tellin' you, something's just not right. I can feel it on the wind. We shouldn't be here... We shouldn't *be* –"

"*Aauauugh!*" came a cry from the back of the group.

"*Shit!*" Rachel cried, jumping a foot off the ground as she spun around frantically. "*Buck!*"

The upper half of Buck's body was gone, consumed by two great reptilian jaws that seemed to blend in with the trees. Blood poured out from the dinosaur's mouth, raining over Buck's pants and down his shirt. Crunching flesh and bone, the dinosaur's serrated teeth punctured Buck's fleshy stomach, making his body writhe and convulse. The more Buck struggled, the tighter the allosaurus' grip compressed, and the further the teeth drove into the helpless victim.

"Where... where did it come from..." was all John could manage to say, walking backwards hesitantly. The three others ran past him, ignoring his dumbfounded remark as they bounded deeper into the foliage, shrieking as they fled.

John couldn't take his eyes off the terrifying scene, imprinting Buck's sudden death in his memory forever. The allosaurus paid the naval veteran little attention, thrashing Bush's body back and forth as the dinosaur struggled to lift the obese dying human off the ground. Then, with an unnatural quick sideways head jerk, John heard a snap within the carnivore's throat, and he knew Buck's neck had broken.

"No! *Gaugh*, I'm sorry, Buck. I'm sorry."

John gasped as Buck's legs stopped moving, going limp as the dinosaur let the heavy body hit the pine-needled earth. His face now a marred mess of serrated tooth puncture marks, Buck was hardly recognizable from the creature's savage mauling.

As the allosaurus bit down on the corpse's neck, it shot John a warning look. Then with a guttural growl as if warning the veteran to stay away from the fresh kill, the dinosaur returned to its feast, savoring every bite.

Run! Run, you asshole.

Breaking free of the creature's dark spell, John spun around, fell flat on his face, and took off after his peers.

4

"What the shit was that?" Dane cursed, slamming his fist against the bark of a conifer. "*It*... it just appeared out of *nowhere* and snatched Buck! The damn thing crunched him in half! How does something like that even happen? How did we not hear it comin'? What kind of monster are we dealing with?"

Hiding under the shade of the late evening sun, the four students regrouped near a wooded area on the edge of a patch of trees. Exhausted and out of breath, they had been running for fifteen minutes off trail and through rugged terrain, until at last all four of them couldn't move any further.

"It's a master hunter, Dane," John replied, arriving in the clearing after being half a minute behind the others from his late start. "It's been hunting in woods like this for millions of years. It's used to getting the jump on its prey."

"But how?" Dane grumbled. "How didn't any of us see it comin'?"

"Simple," Rachel replied, cracking open her canteen and draining the remainder of the contents. "For one, it must walk lighter than it gives off."

"What's that supposed to mean?" Dane remarked, annoyed that he couldn't understand the significance of the statement. "English please, Rachel."

"It means that when we first encountered the allosaurus, it walked loud on purpose, which gave us all a false sense of security in that we could hear it coming a mile away. In reality, it can walk as gentle as any other predator. I'm assuming that 'knocking-over-trees' nonsense was just another false hunting tactic. I'm realizing now that what we're dealing with can be very quiet, without as much as disturbing a single branch as it stalks its prey – us!"

"Right," John elaborated. "And also, based on where we were headed, it knew how to get there faster. After we split from the highlands behind that log, it probably took a short cut, beat us there, and used its camouflaging scales to lie in wait. It picked a spot where it knew we would be comin' through, and that's when it made its move."

"Poor Buck!" Vivian cried, burying her tearful face in her grimy hands. "He never had a chance! Just like Professor Slovak."

"Well that worked in our favor," Dane interjected. "You saw how fat and out of shape Buck was. That dinosaur will be feasting on that bloated carcass all night. Which gives us time to get out of this nightmare for good."

A moment of silence fell over the group, generated by the utter lack of regard for Buck's ill-fated hike.

What an asshole, John thought, trying to find words to express his anger. Rachel beat him to it, speaking first.

"Why don't you show a little sympathy, Dane," Rachel scowled.

"What, Rachel? Were you two *lovers* or something?"

"*No!* But he was our —"

"Then shut the hell up," Dane fired back. "Don't you people get it. It's survival of the fittest out here, honey. Buck was lucky enough that the dinosaur got it over with fast. All that matters is that the four of us are still alive, and if we keep moving, we can keep it that way."

"This isn't Lord of the Flies," John scowled. "You should show some respect for the dead, Dane."

"The hell it ain't!" Dane spat.

"Come on, you two!" Vivian interrupted. "We don't have time for this. The dinosaur is still out there. Sure, we can speculate that maybe it will be... *busy*... with Buck for awhile, but there's no guarantee that will be the case. Now, Alten, how much distance do you think we've put between us and the dinosaur?"

"Maybe two miles," John replied, gulping down his canteen, his Navy shirt drenched in sweat. "I'm not sure how many miles off these things can smell. But as Dane rudely pointed out, it's possible the allosaurus will be with Buck for awhile before it thinks to come after us again — and that's if it even decides to come after us. More than likely, it will head back inland. I'm guessing we are at the edges of its hunting territory, and that it probably keeps to the interior of Red Peak."

"Why do you think that?" Rachel asked.

"Because although the thing is a killing machine, I'm sure it tries to keep to the center of the park to avoid brushes with the public eye. With the multiple intersecting roadways and back roads that run along the park perimeter, it would probably avoid the edges at all costs."

"I remember most of the park disappearances that I've read about tend to happen in the middle of the park versus the outskirts," Rachel remembered. "*Wow,* that's a really sickening feeling knowing what probably happened to all those unfortunate people."

"That's right, sister," Dane said, faking a chomping motion. "Dino-food."

"Your lack of sympathy is appalling, Dane," Vivian frowned, picking pine needles from her hair. "If you had been standing in a different spot, it very easily could've been you that got eaten rather than Buck. I wouldn't make any more jokes about it, if I were you."

"I'll say or do whatever I feel like saying or doing," Dane barked, ignoring the comically redundant statement. "Okay, do y'all think we've breaked here long enough? Suppose that thing has a big appetite and finishes off Buck quicker than I thought. We should get going if we wanna be out of here by dark."

"Now let's think about this for a moment," John said. "I think we follow this path out from the woods. It looks like the path crests a hundred yards up trail. There we should be able to see what's ahead, and hopefully, the outskirts of the park. At the very least, we should be coming up on a back road. That oughta give us a good gauge at how much hustling we have to do before we're out of the woods, no pun intended."

"You *really* think we're close to the edge?" Vivian asked, a glimmer of hope in her voice.

"We have to be," John replied. "I'm willing to wager that up ahead we're gonna see the end of the park. We'll flag down a car and hightail it back to the nearest town. Warn the locals."

With that, the group followed John out from the wooded area. The edge of the tree patch fed through what John guessed had once been an ancient Native American trail. The path led up a rocky grade until the sunlight illuminated the upper crest, as if highlighting the potential viewpoint where they would observe the park limits. Dane pushed past John as they walked up, drawn on by the excitement of finally being rid of the nightmare.

"Move aside, Alten," Dane demanded, rudely brushing past his shoulder. "I have to see! We have to be close. We *have* to be... *ah*, dammit!"

Dane cursed, slamming his fist against a boulder. While the three others trickled in behind him, John couldn't help but bear the same defeating frown, realizing that his assumptions of the park's presumed perimeter was still way off.

Ahead lay a familiar view that they had been encountering since they realized they were lost. Stretching out to the horizon was another series of valleys, mountains, and forests, comprising the entire frame, up until the wooded landscape met with the amber sky. John scanned the bottom of the nearest valley, failing to identify any roads or forest ranger trails.

"Nothing," Vivian whined, whirling around to the others in hysteria. "There's nothing, Alten!"

"Just wait," Rachel assured her. "It's not a great time to panic, Viv.

Listen! Can anyone hear anything? A car? A motorist? Surely there must be something!"

They listened, hearing only the familiar murmur of pine needles as the trees swayed in the summer air. John retrieved a pair of Navy branded tactical binoculars from his backpack and scanned over the scenic landscape. Through the vignetted view ports, all he could find were the amplified images of their same depressing predicament.

"*Anything?*" Rachel asked.

"Nothing," John frowned, lowering the binoculars. "Damn. I was so sure that we'd at least see a ranger station or at the very least, a distant town that we could walk to."

"Shit, Alten!" Dane cursed, throwing a fist in the air dramatically. "It looks like we're even *farther* into the park than we thought we were! By now, who knows where we're at! We could've been walking in circles for all we know."

"No, *no!*" John snapped. "Dane, I'm tellin' you! If we keep going this way, we'll find our way out sooner than any other direction. If we came in from the east, then it has to be the fastest route out."

"But we've been out here for hours," Vivian said, starting to weep again. "How far into the park could we have gotten before we realized we were lost? Maybe by then we were almost on the west end?"

"Let me see that map, Alten," Dane scowled. "If you stay in charge, you'll probably lead us right into the monster's nest! Then we'll all be in for a world of hurt."

"Unlikely, Dane, but here you go. Knock yourself out."

Dane snatched the map from John's hands, while John shot him a disgruntled look.

Take it, you son of a bitch, John thought, fed up with his assigned hiking buddy.

"If you want to be the one to pick the direction out of here," John went on, "be my guest. But I won't be going with you. I'm still heading east. And the longer we sit here questioning my rationale, the longer we're in grave danger."

"Keep your theories to yourself from now on, John," Dane mumbled, as if to dishonor his rival by not using his nickname. "Okay, let's see. Yeah. By now I have literally no idea where anything is. This has to be the worst drawn map I've ever seen of a national park. It all looks the same! There's no identifying characteristics of any area. I can't distinguish anything!"

"How big is the entire park?" Vivian asked.

"Fifty miles in all directions," Dane replied, locating the statistics listed in the upper right corner of the page.

"That's not so bad."

"It's bad, Viv," John said, retying his boot laces. "Fifty miles as the crow flies. We're on the ground. With all the up and down topography and walking around obstacles, it's more than fifty miles for us."

"Try your phone, Viv," Rachel suggested. "We're up high enough now. Maybe you can get service."

"*Ohh*, good idea!" Vivian exclaimed, digging through her backpack for the phone. As she pulled the device out, her hopeful smile faded, as she resumed her look of hopelessness and defeat. "Battery's dead."

"Any luck on that map, Dane?" Rachel asked, peeking over his shoulder.

"What does it look like?" he said, crumpling the map and handing it back to John. "If anyone else wants to take a crack at it, be my guest. But if I were you, I'd be through letting John lead us."

"Interesting," John replied, shoving the map back into his backpack. "And who's gonna pick the new direction out of here, Dane. *You?* Ha. You've gotten lost at least three times before on other class excursions from what I've heard."

"What are you gettin' at?" Dane replied, assuming his position in front of his opponent's face.

"I'm 'getting at', you are a disgrace to forestry and didn't deserve to pass any of the outdoor classes thus far," John smiled, knowing his hurtful comments were sure to inflict maximum pain. "Basically, Dane, you're on track to become the *worst* student in *all* of Montana forestry! Maybe you should just stick to what you're good at – bar fights and toxic, abusive relationships."

"That's it, you scumbag!"

Dane rushed forward, hands balled into fists. As his opponent threw a wild right hook, John stepped aside with ease, executing a quick punch to Dane's unprotected ribs, sending him squealing in pain. Rachel and Vivian backed up as the brawl unfolded on the small plateau, with Dane throwing wild jabs and John countering with simple, strategic counterattacks.

"*Ugh!* Damn you, Alten!" Dane roared, defeated as he vomited over a rock. "By the time we get out of here, this won't be the last time we dance."

"Is that a threat, Dane?"

"You bet, *John*."

"Guys, stop it," Rachel interrupted, stepping between the two combatants. "There isn't time for *thi–* "

From down the trail, two trees toppled over with loud tremors. As the trunks fell and slammed into the earth, the green shape of the allosaurus appeared within the new gap. Stepping onto the sunny path, the theropod locked onto the four figures on the plateau ahead, before letting out a tyrannical growl that echoed around for miles.

"*No!*" Vivian shrieked, stumbling sideways. "*No!*"

"I guess the big son of a bitch finished Buck off early," Dane remarked, his hands shaking in fright.

John felt the crippling fear return into his gut as it crawled up his spine. Behind him, he could hear the three others start to turn to run, even as the allosaurus already began to bound up toward them, jaws spread in a hungry grin.

5

"Run! Run!"

Rachel's shrieks cut through the air as the four graduate students bolted in terror. Following the rugged beaten path around the adjacent side of the slope, John quickly caught up with the others. Refusing to turn around, he could feel the dreadful impact tremors of the allosaurus' feet slamming the plateau, resulting in another challenging roar once the monster reached the summit.

"The *trees!*" Rachel cried. "We need to reach the treeline!"

The trail ended abruptly, giving way to a rocky embankment created by thousands of years of erosion. At the base of the slope over a hundred yards downhill, the first row of pine trees commenced, giving way to another stretch of wild forest. Over his pounding heart, John could hear their colossal pursuer turn down the slope above them, beginning its chase to cut them off from reaching the woodland.

If we don't make it to the trees, we're done for! That thing could get to us much easier out here in the open!

Vivian turned, uttering a petrified yelp before continuing her clumsy descent. The ground was arduously difficult to navigate while running. Uneven rocks gave way to micro avalanches, as the majority of the slope was comprised of pebbles and oddly-shaped minerals a foot in diameter. As John's foot fell through another soft area of loose earth, what he saw made his blood run hot.

To the far left, Dane turned, swiftly elbowing Vivian in the ribs before kicking her shin.

"*Augh!* Dane, you piece of *fu* –"

The ground beneath her legs broke apart in a mess of tumbling pebbles, sending Vivian spiraling to the side. The earth swallowed her left heel, making her fall disgracefully on the slope with her head coming down hard on a rock. Dane smirked heartlessly, continuing undaunted toward the trees.

"Dane! You piece of shit!" John screamed, unable to stop due to pent-up momentum and the skidding movement of rocks under his boot heels.

"Survival of the fittest, Alten!" Dane laughed wickedly, tearing toward the forest. "You'll thank me later!"

"I can't believe you!" Rachel snapped, running several feet ahead of John and also unable to stop her hectic descent. "I *literally* can't believe what you just did!"

Vivian's agonizing cries for help blared like a siren behind them. Dane rushed through the treeline, continuing into the forest like an Olympic runner until he was out of sight.

"What an asshole!" Rachel snapped as Dane's sprinting figure materialized into the shaded trees, out of view.

"He'll get what's comin' to him," John stated, turning back to the slope to behold the horrific scene.

Writhing in terror halfway up the rocky embankment, Vivian crawled out from the section of the hill that gave way after Dane's surprise attack. Gashes from the pebbles left her thighs a scraped ruin of bruises and dirt. She threw her filthy hair over her shoulder, screaming down at the pair below.

"Help me, John!" she screamed, unable to stand. "That bastard twisted my ankle! John, *please!* John, *hel–*"

As her doom closed in from behind her, John surmised from his position that he would be unable to prevent his friend's imminent demise. Vivian turned, accepting her fate as she became consumed by the shadow of the tyrannical reptile.

Skidding down the hillside in a similar clumsy fashion, the allosaurus walked sideways, quickly circumnavigating obstacles and potholes until arriving at Vivian's stagnant destination. Crawling backward as she faced her assailant, Vivian let a final yelp escape her lips as the allosaurus' jaws closed around her torso.

"I... *I* can't watch," Rachel winced, turning into John's shoulder.

Lifting the woman off the ground sideways in its jaws, the allosaurus crunched down on Vivian's waist, splintering her rib cage and pelvis. Vivian screamed only momentarily, succumbing to death shortly after her feet left the earth. Flailing her corpse around like a mad dog with a stick, the allosaurus carelessly tossed her limp body aside, letting Vivian's corpse slam back down on the rocky slope.

"Vivian," Rachel murmured, reciting her dead friend's name. "*Why?* Why is it doing this to us?"

"Because, Rach," John replied, unable to take his eyes off the hillside, "We're trespassers in its territory. It's taking it upon itself to eradicate us. It's not a matter of hunger. It might even have a nest. It's a matter of a territorial animal defending its territory."

The allosaurus gave a victorious growl, lashing its tail back and forth as it walked over to the place where Vivian's body had landed. With a push of its snout, the allosaurus nudged the corpse over, sending Vivian's face turning toward John. Locking eyes with her lifeless stare, he knew she was long gone. Her lips parted briefly; a reflex from the massive carnivore's brute force as the snout rocked her fragile body. Spreading its jaws again, revealing the rows of jagged teeth, the carnivore prepared to deal a second brutal attack to the woman's body as if to confirm its target was dead.

"We should go," John said, stepping into the treeline.

Rachel complied, understanding the severity of John's tone. The pair spun away from the forest's edge away from the hillside, slipping into the shadowy forest. The sudden movement gave pause to the allosaurus as it was about to maul Vivian's body. Then, as if being reminded of its mission to eradicate all territorial infiltrators, the carnivore turned toward the treeline, roaring in fury.

#

"Did you hear that?" Rachel asked, struggling to catch up with the naval veteran. "John, I think it's still coming! How the hell are you planning on outrunning that thing? John, are you listening to me? *Alten? John!*"

John Alten was somewhere else entirely – hellbent on revenge on Dane for what he did to Vivian. Tears of anger welling in his eyes, he scanned the trail ahead until he located Dane's tracks in the moist earth.

The bastard has a good head start on me! I can't let him get away with it. He... he murdered Vivian Perry!

"*John!*" Rachel snapped. "John, stop! I know what you're doing! We don't have time for this. Leave him! We can escape down another way. He'll never find his way out of the park anyway without our help. The dinosaur will pick him off. John, *please!* Focus, this is the last thing we need to be doing right – "

"No, Rachel!" John yelled, pausing his run in mid-stride before turning wildly to his remaining companion. "He murdered Vivian Perry. We all could've gotten away if he didn't do what he did. And worst of all – I did *absolutely* nothing! I just watched it happen and kept running."

"There was nothing you could've done," Rachel assured as she pushed him along the path, shooting a glance over her shoulder. "We were practically tumbling down that hill. If you had gone back for Vivian, you would've been killed too. It's not like you could've saved her, John. The allosaurus was practically on top of us even before Dane pulled his little stunt."

"I don't care, Rach! I have to believe there would've been a chance that she would still be alive. And then what? He just takes off and leaves us to deal with the bloody aftermath?"

"Probably because he knew you'd deck him one," Rachel said, pushing through a low hanging pine branch. "Come on, John. Leave him. He's shown his true colors, not that we all already didn't know he was capable of doing something that evil. When we make it out of here, I'll be telling the authorities about it. He'll go to jail, if he even makes it out alive."

"I'm sorry, Rach," John went on, "but I'm not letting him get off that easy – *shit!*"

"*What?*" Rachel whimpered, paralyzed in fright. "Don't tell me it's already..."

"Yeah," John replied, feeling the cold familiar sting of fear. "I can feel it, just like Vivian sensed when it killed Buck. It's comin' for us..."

A gentle breeze rustled through the branches above them, rattling the pine needles. On the gust of wind, John could smell something nearby; the primordial scent of dried scales – and fresh blood. Grabbing Rachel by the wrist, the pair dashed behind a rocky cleft in the woodland.

"You don't think we should keep running?"

"Haven't decided yet," John replied. "Remember what happened last time? The damn thing already cut us off. Very likely, it could've already moved on ahead of us and found a path to lie in wait. Keep your eyes peeled. Maybe we can still evade it."

Peering over the cleft, John wrestled with his inner fears. Being hunted wasn't something he had experienced – and certainly not from an ancient predator six times his size. The dinosaur had picked off two of his friends, leaving only him and Rachel to fend for themselves, lost in a maze of mountains and forests that was Red Peak National Park. It was a dinosaur of incredible intelligence, using its cunning instincts to herd them into kill-zones, picking them off one by one as it whittled down their confidence and mental sanity.

We have to find a way out of here, John blinked, trying to harness what remaining optimism he had left. *We have to tell the world about this thing...They have to know!*

Turning over his shoulder as if to check if the allosaurus was flanking them, John looked back at the trees ahead. Through the dream-like hypnotic ebb and flow of the branches in the wind, he was only able to see a few birds and a pair of playing squirrels among the underbrush.

That putrid smell... I know it's out there. It's close.

"Rach, maybe we should –"

"*There!*" she interrupted with a frantic whisper, pointing through the foliage.

The branches continued their slow graceful dance along the wind –

and then John saw it. Slinking through the trees almost a hundred yards away, the allosaurus appeared between two trunks, walking in a slow and quiet shuffle. Its large green feet barely making a sound, the dinosaur carefully slithered through the trunks, weaving through them like obstacles in a collision course. Its tail danced back and forth playfully, yet with expert precision, the animal avoided knocking into any trees as it continued its treacherous advance.

"We should leave," Rachel said, looking behind them. "It could be –"

"*Wait!*" John interrupted. "Look. It's heading away from our scent trail. It's moving quickly to cut us off, anticipating where we'll be several miles inland."

John's astute observation was correct. The allosaurus veered away from the trail they had taken to the log, choosing instead to proceed northeast, at a pace that suggested an expedited arrival. A minute later, the creature was out of sight, vanishing into the shades of green and brown that comprised the scenic landscape. When the beast's slithering figure was completely gone, John turned back to Rachel.

"If we keep going down that trail, we're goners," he stated. "We know what's gonna be waiting for us down that way. The best thing to do now is double back a mile or two, then maybe cut north. We need to keep the dinosaur guessing as to where we'll be headed nex –"

Hiding several trees away was Dane Wells. Feeling his expression conform from strategy to rage, John stood up and began to walk toward his colleague. Behind, he could feel Rachel's stare following him, silently pleading to forget about his rival.

I don't care, Rach. He can't get away with this...

"Is it gone?" Dane asked, feigning a look of terror and bewilderment as he poked his bod out from behind his tree.

"Yeah," John replied, proceeding toward Dane. "It's gone."

"*Whew!*" Dane replied, oblivious to John's subtle approach. "Thank God. I thought that thing would never give up, Alten. Hey, looks like Vivian bit the dust back there. Better her than us, I say. Am I right?"

"No, Dane," John replied, his muscles bulging in his sleeves. "She didn't *just* bite the dust. She was murdered. Murdered by you!"

"*Murdered?*" Dane replied. "Are you serious, Alten? It was her or us! I chose *us!* I made a call and I acted on it. We all might be dead now if it wasn't for me, so you're welcome! Asshole."

"No! We would've all made it to the trees. We could've regrouped and come up with a plan there. Instead, you never gave her that chance. She's dead, Dane. Her blood is on your hands."

"Okay, Alten," Dane frowned, balling his fists. "I can see you want to go for round two."

"I thought you'd never ask," John said, moving to attack. "I'm happy to oblige."

6

Brawling wasn't something that John Alten took lightly. During his four years of service to the United States Navy, he had been in a few fights with shipmates. Hell, in his time in high school he had his share of neighborhood mix-ups. More often than not, he tried to avoid physical confrontations altogether. Over the years, he began to discover his muscular build often attracted unwanted attention from other alpha males, forcing him to defend himself and grant the aggressors the battle they so desperately craved. But he was never one to throw the first punch – until now.

After his fist connected with Dane's square jaw, John shook his hand by the wrist. Dane fell backward, his back ramming into a conifer trunk, sending pine needles raining down on his sweat-stained tee shirt.

"Okay, Alten," Dane grumbled, wiping the blood from his lip. "Round two."

Regaining his fighting stance, Dane swung wildly at his opponent – a move John had been counting on. Moving aside with ease, the veteran let his enemy pass by, executing a skillful jab to the neck. The counterattack sent Dane flying once more in the opposite direction, until he braced himself against a log. Then, in an unexpected surprise attack, the brawler extended his back leg, powerfully kicking John in the side.

"*Augh!*" he cried, falling to the side, trying to reach out and grab anything to stabilize himself.

Shit! Wasn't expecting that one...

That gave Dane all the motivation he needed. Leaping up from his crooked posture against the log, he pounced on John, beginning a series of tussles back and forth on the ground. John blocked most of the punches, but knew his opponent had the upper hand by being above him. Rachel tried to push Dane off, but he ignored her, pushing her away effortlessly with a free elbow.

"We don't have time for this!" she pleaded. "That allosaurus could double back! We're wasting time!"

"I tried to tell you, Alten!" Dane grumbled, taking a punch to the chin as he maintained his position above John. "It could've been all of us on that slope! I made a play to keep us alive! If you can't appreciate that, then maybe *you* were the one that deserved to die!"

"You didn't make a play to keep us alive," John grunted, blocking a punch. "You made a play to keep *you* alive!"

John knew he was in trouble. Feeling Dane's bulky weight on top of his chest made it strenuous to breathe, and defending from the brawler's wild right and left hooks was tiresome. Although he had beaten Dane earlier with ease, he knew from stories around campus that he had been the victor in many a fight. And from what John ascertained from his opponent's fighting style, he surmised that Dane was more than adept at adjusting his strategy in order to claim victory.

Just have to get him off me... then I think I can win this...

"I hope that big bastard comes back," Dane smiled with cruel delight, punching John on the side of the cheek. "Then maybe I can just push you down and run for it. Although it might be fun watching it tear you limb from limb. I must confess – I never liked you, John. I always thought – *ugh!*"

John smiled as Rachel's wrist extended around from behind Dane's neck. Latching on like an assassin, she grabbed hold of her wrist with the other hand, entrapping Dane in a choke-hold. Caught off guard and enraged by Rachel's boldness, Dane rose off John's torso. Flailing wildly to throw her off didn't work as well as he hoped. Rachel jumped on his back, latching her thighs around his waist in a tight-grip.

Damn. She must've taken self-defense classes or karate.

Impressed by Rachel's creativity and tenacity, John returned to his feet, gathering himself before preparing his counterattack. Finally, Dane elbowed Rachel in the ribs – a move John guessed that probably happened by sheer luck rather than seasoned skill. Her body slamming on the ground with a defeated shriek, Rachel landed on a bed of pine needles.

"Okay, bitch," Dane said, wiping blood from his mouth as he stood awkwardly over her. "I guess it's time you had some –"

Channeling all of his ferocity and pent-up frustration from the day's horrific events – half of them caused by Dane – John sent his body flying through the air. Extending his leg to position his hiking boot to the front, he connected with Dane's back.

Gotcha, asshole.

"*Yaaha!*" Dane cried out, a tear flying from his eyes as he crumpled to the ground.

His head striking a tree trunk, he fumbled down to the earth, crying in pain as he threw a hand over his shoulder where John had planted his boot. Panting in distress, he cried again as his hand touched the sore spot, moaning unhappily in defeat.

"Are you okay?" John asked, helping Rachel up.

"Yeah. He got me good, but not as good as you got him, it looks like."

"Where did you learn to fight like that?" John asked, brandishing a smile of relief. "That was incredible! You totally saved *my* ass, and kicked *his* ass!"

"When I was young I watched a documentary about the Night-Stalker," she admitted, massaging where Dane hit her. "It made me want to learn self-defense. Took some classes here and there, and my Dad showed me some stuff. He was a ju-jitsu student in his younger days. But most of that I'd say was just improv."

"Well, you 'improv' really well," John smiled, turning back to his defeated opponent.

"*Augh*, Alten," Dane moaned, rubbing his shoulder. "You lunatic. I think you busted something out of place, you piece of shit."

After John's fateful kick, Dane had transformed from a powerful sparring partner to a fragile weak victim, slumped against the old log with his hands up, as if begging for mercy. John was about to resume the attack, but Rachel grabbed his shoulder.

"It's over, Alten," she said. "He's not gonna be of much trouble anymore. I say we leave him and keep heading in the direction we were going, adjusting course to avoid the allosaurus down the road. The sun's setting, but we still have some time. We could still make it out by nightfall."

"I think it's a little late for that," John replied, subtly grabbing her by the wrist.

"Why's *tha* –"

Rachel turned pale, carefully backing away from the log. From behind Dane's shoulder, a large green shape began to emerge from behind the dense pine branches. Rustling the final branch away with an enormous pointed snout, the allosaurus revealed itself to the trio of survivors, letting a gentle rumble escape its jaws as the great shadow flooded over Dane.

"Hey, what's *tha – oh no*, Alten. Please, Alten! Do something! We can talk about this... I'm sorry man, *seriously!* Dude, come on..."

"Back away carefully," John replied, pressing his palm into Rachel's waist as they backed away discreetly, relieved that the carnivore focused its gaze solely on Dane.

"*Alten!*" Dane whined helplessly, struggling to stand up as the allosaurus placed a massive foot on the log, moving its toothy grin toward its prey.

"It's like you said, Dane," John said, shuffling backwards, flashing a smile. "Survival of the fittest."

"Alten please, look man. You were right. I messed up. Do

something, dude! *Auugh! AuUuUgh!*"

Letting off a menacing hiss that reminded John of an agitated Nile crocodile, the allosaurus clamped its jaws around Dane's upper torso. His screams barely audible from within the carnivore's jaws, Dane twisted and convulsed within the monster's powerful grip, even as his feet left the ground.

"Come on," John heard Rachel say, tugging at his sleeve. "We still have a chance. While it's busy..."

"Yeah," John muttered, shooting one last look at the dinosaur before sprinting after his colleague.

In the clearing behind them, the allosaurus crunched down on Dane's neck, sending blood gushing down the victim's torso, ending the futile struggle. With an apathetic gurgle, the carnivore let the body slide out from the jaws, crashing on the pine needle floor, before sending a challenging roar echoing throughout Red Peak National Park.

Then remembering its mission, the allosaurus took off down the trail-head, realizing there were still two targets left.

Dane's body remained where it lay, lifeless, unrecognizable, and alone.

#

"Keep going!" John cried, firmly striking his shoulder on a coarse rocky surface as he swerved around the woodland trail. "I think it's still coming!"

"Alten," Rachel panted. "Seriously, I don't think I can go on much longer. I need a break."

"I know," John gasped, leaning forward and holding his kneecaps. "I'm not doing too great myself..."

Since the allosaurus had annihilated its last victim – whom John dubbed 'the asshole formerly known as Dane' – they had maintained a course due northeast. Following that course with what could be best described as an exhausted, ceaseless jog, even John was beginning to feel the effects of fatigue and dehydration. Both of them had depleted their water-supply, craving a drink or, at the very least, a respite in peace without the threat of their relentless, primordial pursuer.

But it's still coming. It's basically a robot on a mission. Destroy the territorial invaders – at all costs...

"This is nuts," Rachel said, her voice teetering on delirium as she collapsed on a severed trunk. "How much longer can we keep this up? Maybe it'd be better if we climb one of these trees and wait it out."

"Come on, Rach," John urged, pulling her up by the wrist. "That won't work. It will just wait us out until we die from dehydration. We're better off continuing onward."

"It'll be dark soon," she added, hustling behind him as he continued to press ahead through the thicket. "We'll never see that thing coming, Alten."

John swallowed hard, his throat dry and craving water as he realized the horrible reality of Rachel's observation. By now, the sun was setting over the distant peaks in the opposite direction, flooding them in the last remaining haze of sun. Above in the treetops, constellations of stars were already gracing the sky with their glistening brilliance. Soon, the only light they would have would be the subtle glow of moonlight.

"Damn," John swore, looking around as he tried to fight off a panic attack. "Okay, let's just think. *Augh.* We're still in this, Rach! Don't give up. Think. We have to be getting close to the edge of the park. We have to be —"

"Alten, *there!*"

"What? The allosaurus?"

"*No!* Through those trees. See it?"

"Holy crap, Rach! You bet your ass I see it!"

John could hardly believe his eyes. At first, he thought what Rachel may have been pointing at was a mirage brought on by delirium. But when he realized they were both seeing the same object, he cast aside his doubts.

Nestled through the grove of pine trees ahead was the very top of a park ranger watch tower. A few quick steps ahead revealed that the tower was connected to a service building at the bottom of a slope, not more than a five minute hike down the wooded embankment. A single Jeep was parked beside the building, and lights from the inside spilled out onto the grassy trail to the building forefront, indicating there were most likely park rangers stationed inside.

"Rach!" John exclaimed, hugging his friend. "I think you might have saved us!"

"Well don't celebrate yet," Rachel smiled as they started down the hill. "We haven't made it down this steep cliff and —"

Less than a mile behind them through the trees, an aggressive, dominant roar rippled through the branches, sending bats and crows flying up from the treetops, blocking out the stars. The roar was quickly followed by thunderous footsteps — footsteps that very quickly transitioned from a dramatic walk to a full-on sprint through the dark countryside.

"It's comin'!" John yelled as they both took off down the hill.

It's not trying to sneak around anymore. It knows we're almost out of the park! It's coming straight for us!

"Go, Rach! *Gooo!*"

7

"We'll keep an eye out, boss," Ranger Donny Walters said into the microphone of his radio set. "Until then, we'll let you know if anything changes. Over and out."

Donny clicked off his microphone and settled back into his worn-out leather office chair, eyeing the bland, single room of the ranger outpost station.

Working at nights in the ranger station wasn't something he looked forward to. For one, driving up in the Red Peak trails in the dark had often resulted in near misses with nocturnal wildlife. He had filed a request to get some decent lighting along the ranger access routes, but the form had been sitting on his supervisor's desk unfulfilled since last year, collecting dust in the same place that he delivered it. Not to mention the long hours, unpaid overtime, and random requests to go off into the woods searching for missing people.

That's gotta be the worst part of the job...

Park disappearances in Red Peak had been growing steadily worse since Donny's first day on the job. At first, he thought nothing of the missing persons reports mounting throughout the vast park interior. Sure, hikers go missing all the time, right? Sure. But in Red Peak, people eventually turn up, but never in one piece.

That, of course, was a part the park service kept from the public.

A shudder crept up Donny's shoulders when he remembered the bloody appendages of a hiker that went missing six months ago – Sandy Phillips. Her ravaged corpse had been torn limb from limb. The search team had only recovered her head and her right arm, both of which had been crudely severed by some form of savage animal attack.

But what type of animal? It's anyone's guess at this point.

The disappearances and slayings in the park brought on numerous questions by the park employees – was it some kind of large bear doing this? Bears were prevalent in the park, but there was no evidence of bears present when the bodies were recovered. Mountain lions? Same deal.

What is it? What's out there?

Donny Walters pondered the question many a night, and this night was no different, especially now that his boss, Paul, had reported that several cars on the eastern parking lot had been vacant past park closing.

Sitting in the park ranger office with his co-worker, Sarah Johnson, Donny stood up from his rickety chair and retrieved his fresh brewed coffee, from a pot he assumed would soon go faulty.

"What do you think of it?" he asked, sipping from the mug with a sunny Red Peak logo on it.

"Think of what?" Sarah asked, tying her red hair into a tight pony tail.

"You know. Everything. The disappearances. These five or six missing people that we've been told about today."

"Your guess is as good as mine, Donny," Sarah replied, popping her bubble gum. "I used to think there was a Bigfoot loose in the park. I'm just glad they've finally brought on some fresh employees and enforcement to help sort it all out. Plus now that the government is involved... Sometimes it's creepy working out here in the woods knowing all that's been going on. Not gonna lie, I've thought about quitting several times. It's hard to handle, you know? Every late night I'm told I'm working out here, it leaves me thinking there's some big creature watching us – waiting for me to step outside and –"

The door to the entrance burst open, roughly striking the corner of the wall as two dark figures stormed into the room – a man and a woman. The woman, who looked young enough to be Donny's daughter, ran to the back of the room, hiding behind the reception desk. The man swerved around to the entrance, slamming the door shut and locking the deadbolt before meandering over to the window, peeking through the tacky office blinds.

"Hey, are you – "

"John Alten," the man replied hastily, parting several blinds before twisting strings, closing the panels to the outside view. "This is Rachel Robinson. Yes, we're the missing people you're probably looking for. Now, get your supervisor on the horn – the head ranger, ranger general – whatever the hell it's called! Your boss. We *need* backup, *now!*"

"*Whoa*, calm down, son," Donny said, spilling coffee on his forest green shirt in the excitement. "Where have you fellas been? Where are the *othe* –"

"*Dead!*" the girl named Rachel interrupted. "Dead. *All* of them."

"What happened?" Sarah asked, rubbing Rachel's shoulder, her voice faltering in fright.

"It was a dinosaur," John answered, closing another set of blinds. "Allosaurus, I believe. It picked them off one by one. We were lost in the heart of the park when we encountered it, probably damn well encroached on the big bastard's territory. I know it sounds ludicrous, but it's *all* true! And now it's coming this way! Call your people! We need every able body up here to take this thing on. *Guns!* Bring guns!"

"A dinosaur?" Donny choked back a laugh. "This sounds like another Bigfoot ghost story, eh, Sarah?"

"I don't know, Donny," she replied. "Something's clearly rattled them. And you remember those loud roars we hear every once in awhile; we always joked that it was a T-Rex, but truthfully I always thought it was a large reptile. Have you forgotten those big tracks we saw last month? I said it looked like a big crocodile and you laughed at me."

"We're not bull-shitting you," Rachel added. "It's a dinosaur. It's killed four of us already. We're the only two left alive. If you don't believe us, then fine! But *please*, make the damn call!"

"Okay, okay," Donny said, avoiding Rachel's sharp eye contact as he settled back in the chair. "I bet Paul is gonna laugh about this."

He flipped on his microphone and adjusted the speaker knobs on the radio. He could feel the three others gathering around him. John and Rachel – the newcomers – looked just as startled as they had been when they arrived.

Something's definitely got em' creeped out, Donny thought, fidgeting in the chair. *But a dinosaur? If this is a prank by the other park rangers, I swear...*

"Hey boss, it's Don. You won't believe it. There's some good news and some bad news. We found two of the survivors listed as missing. Bad news is that they're saying the other four missing people are – *uhm*, deceased. And *uhm* – they say there's a dinosaur chasing them and supposedly it's on its way to this station as we speak. I know that last part is a little ridiculous, but that's what they're saying. Over."

The man named John leaned in, expecting a quick response. Donny leaned back, trying to hide his smirk about the absurd accusations of prehistoric wildlife running amok in the park. Finally, a reply hummed through the speakers.

"Stay put and lock the doors. We'll be up there in fifteen minutes. Whatever you do, don't leave the safety of the cabin. Over and out."

The cryptic phrase cast an eerie silence over the room. Donny watched as Sarah's face went from uncertainty to terror. Even the muscular man named John, whom Donny guessed was a former armed serviceman, looked more alarmed. He could feel his coffee burning a hole in his stomach, causing him to loosen his belt to relieve the pressure.

"*I...* I think I'm gettin' sick," Donny moaned, padding his beer belly as he searched his desk drawer for medicine. "I need a Pepto. What did he mean by that?"

"Somethin's up, Don," Sarah whispered, her skin ghostly pale. "He told us not to leave? What does he know? What does he know that none of us do? *Aughh!* What's that?"

Shaking several objects in the room, an underground tremor rattled through the park service building. Donny's coffee rippled in his mug, strong enough to coalesce his creamer with the decaf blend. Rachel spun around, eyes wide with fear as her fingernails dug into the corner of Donny's desk.

"*Wha...* what was that?"

"We tried to tell you people," John replied to Sarah. "It's an allosaurus!"

Donny felt himself jump as a deep reptilian guttural growl sounded from the other side of the door. From under the one-inch clearance, a pair of shadows appeared, growing large until they filled the threshold of the entrance. With each monstrous step, the animal maneuvered its bulky head to the gap in the door. Sniffing violently, the creature sent a nauseating breath under the entrance. Donny noted the animal's large green scales on the nostril before the reptile retreated its snout from the opening, vanishing from view.

"What the hell, Don?" Sarah muttered, her teeth chattering as she backed away further. "No one told us when we were stationed up here that we might have to deal with something like *this!*"

"I doubt they knew," Donny replied, shaking in fright. "Either that, or they didn't want to detract potential park visitors from arriving. Suddenly it *all* makes sense! The disappearances. The body parts. This animal must have been responsible!"

"But we should be safe in here, right?" Rachel asked. "I mean, this is like a big fancy ranger station? Don't you have guns?"

"This is just a communications junction," Donny replied, rising up from his chair as he locked the rest of the windows. "Not an armory."

"Maybe we can get in the Jeep and make for the edge of the park," Sarah replied. "It's only another ten miles down the hill. Screw staying put and waiting for backup. If they know what's waiting for them up here, what's stopping them from just leaving us stranded here until they think it's left the area?"

"We'll never make it," John replied. "This thing is a killer; adept at hunting and camouflage. We'll be dead before we set foot outside the door. It's waiting for us just outside, waiting for us to make a move or slip up. *Hey!* Get away from that window!"

Beginning to scream only to catch herself a second later, Sarah sidestepped away from the window – just as a large toothy shadow rolled past in silhouette. The silhouetted animal paused on the other side of the glass, although the occupants were unable to make out any details of the creature due to the thick tan interior curtain. The creature's jaws parted in shadow, proceeding another dreadful growl before the beast hobbled past the window. With a final flick of the tail, the animal was out of view again, flooding the cabin once again in eerie silence.

"This is too much," Sarah whined, diving into Donny's chair as she frantically flicked on the archaic radio. "I'm calling him back! He needs to get here *fast –*"

"Get out of that chair!" John commanded, "You're too close to that window –"

All too quickly, Sarah realized her mistake.

"AUGHHH!"

The window behind her erupted into an explosion of glassy shards as a massive snout broke through the barrier. Raining down glassy shards on the floor, the allosaurus' massive head pushed through the tan tarp, making its ugly reptilian appearance known to the room. In seconds, the massive predator was barreling down on Sarah's position. Fear kept the park ranger rooted in the rickety chair, making Sarah a convenient target for the Jurassic predator.

"Sarah!" Rachel screamed. "Move! Move!"

The allosaurus pushed through the large window, damaging the trim and wall as its bulky form miraculously managed to fit into the room. Sarah instinctively put up her hands as a shield, as little more than a squeal escaped her lips. A growl signaling the imminent attack, the allosaurus spread its jaws wide – enveloping the upper half of Sarah in one powerful chomp.

"Oh my God!" Donny cried, stumbling backwards past the two hikers.

"Where are you going?" John asked.

"The watchtower!" Donny replied, unlocking a door near the back of the room. "It won't be able to get us up there. The stairs are too thin. Well don't just stand there – *come on!*"

Raining blood down on the hardwood floor of the ranger station, the dinosaur lifted Sarah's lifeless lower half off the ground. Its serrated teeth crunching down on bone, the ferocious carnivore hurled the remains across the room. Sarah's severed waist and legs struck the wall with an abrupt bang before falling back to the ground, her boots clattering wildly off the floor. Its recent foe vanquished, the allosaurus turned toward the three remaining occupants, taking a step in their direction as its toe-claws raked over the floorboards, scuffing the glossy finish.

"Go, Rach!" John urged as the pair rushed past Donny, bolting up the metal steps of the watchtower. "Don't look back!"

Donny took one last look at the murderous reptile that just slaughtered his friend. His eyes struggling to make sense of what transpired, Donny eventually likened the image to a more life-like adaptation of a Ray Harryhausen stop-motion monster. But Donny knew those types of monsters only existed in big-budget Hollywood films – a reality that had been shattered in the past five minutes.

But this is real. It's all real!

With a face gnarled in scales that reminded him of some type of bipedal alligator, and razor-sharp claws that weaponized the beast's arms, Donny found himself under the same spell that Sarah had been under. His mind told him to run – run up the same flight of stairs that John and Rachel had climbed, but his feet refused to comply. Instead he was forced to wait in crippling terror as the allosaurus inched closer and closer with each step, until the aisles of reptilian teeth encompassed his vision, and his world went dark.

8

John froze on the first landing of the stairwell, the sound of splintering bones making him turn. Fifteen feet below was the rear entrance of the ranger station, where Donny's silhouette remained frozen in time. Masked under herculean Jurassic jaws, the upper half of the ranger's figure convulsed in a death struggle. Blood rained down from somewhere within the creature's throat, drizzling over Donny's once pristine green ranger outfit.

"*Don –*"

"It's too late, Alten!" Rachel cried, grabbing her friend by the collar. "Come on!"

Ripping the ranger apart like it had done with Sarah only a minute earlier, the allosaurus heaved Donny's bulky form inches off the ground, before carelessly tossing the corpse out of view somewhere inside the ranger station. Turning back toward the rear entrance as if on a mission, the carnivore lumbered out of the opening. Once again, the allosaurus fit through the doorway, managing to only damage one side of the door frame as its serpent-like figure slipped out into the glow of the moonlight.

Staring at the slinking lizard below through the metal mesh grating of the watch-tower stairs, John pounded after Rachel. Turning ahead at the second landing, John saw her look down and gasp, before clumsily continuing her reckless ascent.

To his horror, the allosaurus had begun climbing the stairwell after them. Sniffing at the corroded rusted metal steps, the dinosaur easily confirmed that both humans had fled up the ramp. As John rounded another bend, he reassessed the carnivore's position, horrified to see through the mesh that the allosaurus had begun to ascend the stairs.

"*Augh!*" Rachel shrieked, pointing below. "Beneath us!"

"*WHOA!*"

One level below them, the allosaurus reached the first landing. Sensing its targets were one level up, the carnivore turned its head skyward – just as John and Rachel reached their own landing above. Then, in a precise powerful leap, the allosaurus rammed the ceiling with its bulky scalp, shaking John and Rachel's floor platform.

"Grab hold, Rach!" John shrieked. "It's coming loose!"

Feeling the world drop below his feet as bolts and rivets came loose from the floor grid, John pushed Rachel forward, granting her more momentum to easily reach the final turn on the stairwell, while simultaneously sabotaging his own chances.

"*Augh!*"

As the floor panel dropped out from below his feet, John let his arms flail wildly, battling for any extra inch that his wild jump would earn him. Beside him, he could see the railing shattering apart, the metallic pieces raining down to the ground beside the ranger station. Growling in agony one level below, the allosaurus shrieked as its own floor landing broke asunder, as did the various other parts of the lower stairwell. Crumbling under the dinosaur's immense weight, the allosaurus' chances of getting to the top were dashed as the remnants of the lower staircase were in complete disarray.

"*Ohhh!*" John cried, relieved when his hands reached around the remaining stairwell landing as his feet dangled helplessly. As he threw his legs around the railing and prepared to board the final stairwell until they reached the top of the watch-tower, John looked down. The allosaurus had already dropped back to the forest floor, only to stand back up and jump.

"*Whoa!*" John cried, his heart palpitating wildly as the dinosaur's jaws snapped shut within inches of his foot before the dinosaur fell back to the earth.

"Quit dickin' around, Alten!" Rachel yelled, having already reached the top observatory platform of the watch-tower. "Here, I'm coming down to get *yo–*"

"*No, Rach!* Stay where you're at. This stairwell's set to collapse. It's only a few steps... I think I can make it!"

John swung himself over the railing, landing roughly on the fifth step from the top. The foundation of the final stairwell shaking, he bolted up the remainder of the stairs as the last rivets in place shook loose. His boot touching down on the safety of the upper watch-tower platform, John grabbed Rachel's outstretched hand, seconds before the upper staircase dropped to the ground.

"Close call, Alten," Rachel remarked, wincing as she looked down at the chaos some forty feet below.

"You can say that again," John replied, wiping the sweat from his brow.

Standing on the twenty-foot-wide platform on top of the watch-tower, the pair stared down at the ground below. Among the rubble of the collapsed metal girders that previously formed the watch-tower steps, the allosaurus was lying still, slumped on its side. From the security lights of the ranger outpost building, John could make out the glint of a small red cylindrical object lodged in the dinosaur's neck scales.

A tranquilizer dart?

The slamming of a vehicle door made them look back at the front of the ranger station. Silhouetted from the security lights, four uniformed park personnel exited a pair of green Jeeps. A bulky man in tight-fitting ranger clothes walked at the front, carrying what looked like an elephant tranquilizer gun. When he arrived at the foot of the unconscious allosaurus, the man paused, taking off his safari hat in awe of the large unconscious dinosaur.

"Well, I'll be dammed. Rick, Jamie, you all have to see this! We finally got the elusive son of a bitch!"

"Excuse me," Rachel called from up on the platform. "*Uhm*, thank you for saving our lives. But can you kindly get us down from here?"

The leader of the park rangers laughed, sipping from an exotic-looking canteen.

"*Ha-ha!* There's finally some survivors that can shed some light on all this. You betcha, missy. Rick, I think there should be a ladder in the ranger station. Let's get these folks down. I'm eager to hear their story."

#

The olive-army colored lowboy trailer lumbered up the dirt path into the parking lot in front of the dimly lit ranger station. As the massive vehicle parked, three more U.S. Army branded supply trucks followed behind, parking beside the entrance to the outpost. As the engines to the trucks clicked off, the tarps behind the beds were flung open, spilling at least a dozen armed soldiers per truck out onto the clearing as they darted over to the watch-tower.

Holy shit! We're mixed up in some heavy stuff.

John Alten watched the surreal scene from the comfort of the ranger station lobby, sipping on a fresh pot of coffee. In the allosaurus' attack, surprisingly, the coffee pot wasn't damaged, although the rest of the room was left in ruin.

Beside him, Rachel sat on the couch, trying not to watch as soldiers laid tarps over Donny and Sarah's gruesome remains. Concealing the grisly evidence helped John to feel less squeamish, although the coverings didn't mask the many spatter points of fresh blood throughout the room.

"Perhaps you'd be more comfortable talking outside," the main forest ranger, who had introduced himself as Paul said, folding his arms to reveal his huge biceps.

"No, here's fine," Rachel replied. "I don't know if there's more of those things out there. As much as I hate being in here, I'd rather be inside the station than anywhere out near the treeline."

"And I understand that," Paul replied, setting his safari hat on Donny's table as he brushed aside wood chips and drywall fragments from the dinosaur's siege. "You both have been through a terrible ordeal. Care to share the details?"

"Like what?" John asked.

"Well, for starters, how about where you first encountered the creature?"

"It was about mid-day," John replied. "We had been walking around the park since early morning. We got lost near the middle of the park looking for our class professor. There were five of us. Eventually we found him – ripped to pieces. We didn't know what to make of it, but we saw the tracks and knew it was something big. Right around that area – again, I'm not sure where, but somewhere near the park's interior – it began hunting us. We could hear its roars from far away, but later we determined it was just an act. The allosaurus can actually move very stealthily – a tactic it used to bring about the deaths of our first friend, Buck. Soon after, it killed Vivian and Dane. Rach and I made it here. Donny and Sarah called you, but then it attacked immediately after, killing them too. Donny gave his life so we could make it to the watch-tower. That's where you found us, before you tranquilized the animal."

"And you seem to think it's an *allosaurus*?"

"Yes," John answered in confidence. "I'm quite sure. Looks exactly like the skeleton in the Montana Museum."

"We've been dealing with this issue for some time," Paul admitted, "but we didn't really know what to believe. There were legends in this area dating back a hundred years of a strange lizard that stalked people in Red Peak in the early 1900s. Every once in awhile, tracks would show up mysteriously, but part of me always thought they were hoaxes, you know, fake imprints made by pranksters. Then about a year ago, a family called in a frenzy saying that during one of their hikes here, they saw something straight out of a dinosaur movie. That *really* sparked my attention – they said they were so shook up that they would never come back again. Now I'm seeing that, all along, the stories in Red Peak were true."

"So what happens to it now?" Rachel asked.

"The U.S. Army has had a claim on it," Paul answered. "They've been watching Red Peak with interest ever since these stories surfaced. Believe it or not, they've actually done several sweeps of the park over the years, under the guise of locating missing people, but I've always thought they were going after the mystery creature. But regardless, all of their searches turned up nothing."

"Not surprising," John said. "Given the animal's hunting abilities and camouflaging scales, they could've walked right by the allosaurus several times without even noticing."

"Sir," interrupted one of the younger rangers, moving uneasily past a pair of soldiers that carted off Sarah's remains on a tarp. "Here are the requested forms you asked for."

"Thank you, Jamie," Paul replied as the younger man handed over paperwork before returning to help the army soldiers outside. "These are confidentiality agreements. You both will be required by state law to sign these. It basically states that you have no knowledge about what happened here tonight – and that you'll say nothing about the allosaurus."

"Are you joking?" Rachel asked. "Even if we agree not to tell anyone, how are we gonna explain what happened to our friends? People are gonna ask questions, Paul."

"Just follow in line with the official statement that will be formally announced tomorrow in the papers," Paul replied, handing them both a hastily written press release scribbled on notepaper.

"Four found dead after horrific fall from Red Peak mountains," John read over the lines. "Two survivors made it out after getting lost, then ran into a ranger station, where they told rangers the full details of what happened."

"The rest of the details are up to you," Paul replied. "We're deciding to keep it somewhat vague. So long as you mention nothing about animal predation, you should be covered."

"And if we don't keep quiet?" Rachel asked.

"Well, I can't speak for the army," Paul replied, "but I'm sure you don't want the full force of Uncle Sam's legal resources coming down on you. As for the park service, you'll be fined a substantial amount, because we'll have to cover our asses when the army finds out the public leaked what happened on our grounds. To put it bluntly, you have everything to lose by opening your mouths. Forget about what happened here."

A mechanical whine made John turn to the window. In the clearing outside the front of the ranger station, two fork lifts and a bulldozer had arrived. Working in unison, the three vehicles managed to move the large unconscious dinosaur onto the lowboy trailer bed. With a loud thud, the creature landed on the vehicle. Seconds after the tail flopped over the side, ten soldiers dashed over to the edges of the bed, tossing over cables and tarps, concealing and securing the dinosaur onto the massive truck.

"What are they gonna do with it?" Rachel replied.

"We didn't ask," Paul said, watching the event from the next window. "Whatever it is, they're keeping it very hush-hush."

The lights from the lowboy trailer turned on as the engine jump-started with a roar. The farthest supply truck backed up, acting as a lead vehicle in the convoy. Silhouetted soldiers scurried past the windows, jumping into the back of the adjacent canvas-covered supply truck beds. Giving a curt thumbs up, the driver of the lead truck began to drive away down the dark forest path, with the lowboy following and the two other trucks bringing up the rear.

"They're leaving," Jamie said, coming through the door. "They said they'll be back next week for the bulldozer and the forklifts. Man, how the hell are we gonna clean all this up? And what are we gonna tell Sarah and Donny's families? We're in a world of shit, boss."

"Well we gotta figure something out fast," Paul replied, staring over the disheveled room. "Last thing we need is the army coming back pissed about how we handled it. Speakin' of which, did you two sign those documents?"

"Yeah," John said, collecting Rachel's paper before handing both over to Paul. "We'll keep our mouths shut. But if you have any communication with the army, you have to warn them. This thing *has* to be destroyed! It's a menace, and it only wants one thing – to taste human flesh. If it escapes, I'm telling you; more will die. It won't just be on the army's hands – it'll be *yours* too. Then the secret about what happened here will have to come out."

Paul stared back with a stern grimace, assessing whether Alten had meant it as advice or a threat. Finally, he folded the confidentiality forms into his backpack before heading for the entrance.

"Well, Mr. Alten," he said, grabbing the doorknob. "Let's pray that doesn't happen, for both our sakes. Honestly, I'm hoping the damn lowboy falls off a cliff and that monster is destroyed once and for all, for all the trouble it's caused me over the years. Jamie, Rick. There's some mops and brooms in the closet. Do your best to have this place somewhat sterilized by morning. I've already canceled all shifts tomorrow and the park will be closed due to repairs, which technically *isn't* a lie. Okay, let's go, you two. I'll drive you both back to the city. With any luck, I'll be able to get at least some sleep tonight."

John and Rachel followed Paul out from the building. As John buckled his seat belt in the backseat of Paul's Jeep, his hands enclosed around the large allosaurus tooth in his pocket. The object was so sharp that it sliced part of his fingertip.

This is all the proof I'll ever need. And when it comes time to go public with this story, I know I'll be able to back up my claims. There's families that will need closure, and the world deserves to know what happened out here today... and what's been happening in Red Peak for a hundred long years.

John smiled in relief as Rachel and Paul sat down in front of him, grateful as the Jeep began to coast down the road that fed out of Red Peak.

THE END

Don't forget to leave an honest review of this book on Amazon.com and Goodreads.com. Reviews help writers get noticed which will help reach more readers.

CHECK OUT OTHER GREAT DINOSAUR BOOKS

PRIMORDIA
by **Greig Beck**

Ben Cartwright, former soldier, home to mourn the loss of his father stumbles upon cryptic letters from the past between the author, Arthur Conan Doyle and his great, great grandfather who vanished while exploring the Amazon jungle in 1908.

Amazingly, these letters lead Ben to believe that his ancestor's expedition was the basis for Doyle's fantastical tale of a lost world inhabited by long extinct creatures. As Ben digs some more he finds clues to the whereabouts of a lost notebook that might contain a map to a place that is home to creatures that would rewrite everything known about history, biology and evolution.

But other parties now know about the notebook, and will do anything to obtain it. For Ben and his friends, it becomes a race against time and against ruthless rivals.

In the remotest corners of Venezuela, along winding river trails known only to lost tribes, and through near impenetrable jungle, Ben and his novice team find a forbidden place more terrifying and dangerous than anything they could ever have imagined.

PANGAEA EXILES
by **Jeff Brackett**

Tried and convicted for his crimes, Sean Barrow is sent into temporal exile—banished to a time so far before recorded history that there is no chance that he, or any other criminal sent back, has any chance of altering history.

Now Sean must find a way to survive more than 200 million years in the past, in a world populated by monstrous creatures that would rend him limb from limb if they got the chance. And that's just his fellow prisoners.

The dinosaurs are almost as bad.

CHECK OUT OTHER GREAT DINOSAUR BOOKS

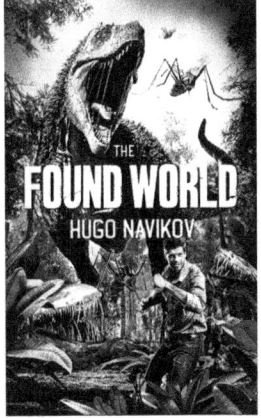

THE FOUND WORLD
by Hugo Navikov

A powerful global cabal wants adventurer Brett Russell to retrieve a superweapon stolen by the scientist who built it. To entice him to travel underneath one of the most dangerous volcanoes on Earth to find the scientist, this shadowy organization will pay him the only thing he cares about: information that will allow him to avenge his family's murder.

But before he can get paid, he and his team must enter an underground hellscape of killer plants, giant insects, terrifying dinosaurs, and an army of other predators never previously seen by man.

At the end of this journey awaits a revelation that could alter the fate of mankind ... if they can make it back from this horrifying found world.

HOUSE OF THE GODS
by Davide Mana

High above the steamy jungle of the Amazon basin, rise the flat plateaus known as the Tepui, the House of the Gods. Lost worlds of unknown beauty, a naturalistic wonder, each an ecology onto itself, shunned by the local tribes for centuries. The House of the Gods was not made for men.

But now, the crew and passengers of a small charter plane are about to find what was hidden for sixty million years.

Lost on an island in the clouds 10.000 feet above the jungle, surrounded by dinosaurs, hunted by mysterious mercenaries, the survivors of Sligo Air flight 001 will quickly learn the only rule of life on Earth: Extinction.

Check out other great

Sea Monster Novels!

C.J. Waller

PREDATOR X

When deep level oil fracking uncovers a vast subterranean sea, a crack team of cavers and scientists are sent down to investigate. Upon their arrival, they disappear without a trace. A second team, including sedimentologist Dr Megan Stoker, are ordered to seek out Alpha Team and report back their findings. But Alpha team are nowhere to be found – instead, they are faced with something unexpected in the depths. Something ancient. Something huge. Something dangerous. Predator X

Robert J. Stava

NEPTUNES RECKONING

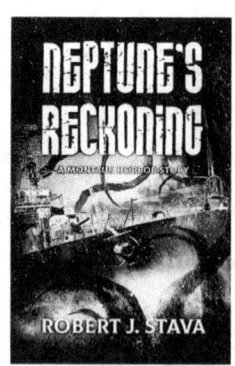

At the easternmost end of Long Island lies a seaside town known as Montauk. Ground Zero on the Eastern seaboard for all manner of conspiracy theories involving it's hidden Cold War military base, rumors of time-travel experiments and alien visitors... For renowned Naval historian William Vanek it's the where his grandfather's ship went down on a Top Secret mission during WWII code-named "Neptune's Reckoning". Together with Marine Biologist Daniel Cheung and disgraced French underwater explorer Arnaud Navarre, he's about to discover the truth behind the urban legends: a nightmare from beyond space and time that has been reawakened by global warming and toxic dumping, a nightmare the government tried to keep submerged. Neptune's Reckoning. Terror knows no depth

www.ingramcontent.com/pod-product-compliance
Lightning Source LLC
Chambersburg PA
CBHW061244170626
46809CB00007B/2831